SWEET LITTLE LIES

LEAH CUPPS

INKUBATOR
BOOKS

Published by Inkubator Books
www.inkubatorbooks.com

Copyright © 2025 by Leah Cupps

ISBN (eBook): 978-1-83756-490-3
ISBN (Paperback): 978-1-83756-491-0
ISBN (Hardback): 978-1-83756-492-7

PROLOGUE

It's often said that just before death, people experience flashes of their entire life—a burst of colorful memories ranging from childhood to first love to family.

But for me? *All I can see is white.*

Bouquets of fragrant lilies, their pure white petals intertwined with delicate pale roses and clusters of baby's breath. White tablecloths that billow like clouds against a gleaming marble floor. A transparent, almost ethereal veil floating over a silky white gown. Borrowed pearls. Strappy white heels. And in the center of it all, a multitiered wedding cake adorned with sugary flour and lace, mocking me with its sickly sweet perfection as I gasp for my last breath.

It's not fair! I want to scream, but my strength has deserted me, leaving the words to die silently on my lips. It's unfair, lying here with my blood pooling around me, knowing that I'll never witness the wedding that consumed my every waking moment.

Weddings are funny like that. It starts off with the seed

of an idea. The two of you reciting your heartfelt vows in front of a few close friends and family. You picture a quaint ceremony with, maybe, fifty loved ones. But, before you know what's happening, RSVPs have ballooned to two hundred guests. Aunt Beth shows up with her seven wayward children. And what about Amy, your second cousin on your dad's side? Couldn't she come and bring her husband and twins? Of course you say yes. Because how could you deprive anyone of joining in this joyful day, celebrating this pinnacle moment of your life?

Suddenly, the simple, heartfelt affair you envisioned morphs into an entirely different beast. A beast that, if you're not careful, can completely consume your life. I let the wedding beast consume my life. Now, I see that was a mistake. *But damn it, it's too late.* The deposits have been made, the DJ paid in full. And now I'm going to die and everyone will eat the cake I spent a thousand dollars on without me. They'll be knocking back the fancy champagne I had shipped in from God-knows-where, all while a single question begins to dawn on them, spreading through the crowd like wildfire:

What happened to the bride?

She's there too, in my vision. The woman whose name hung in the air between us, a silent reminder of everything I was not. It's partially her face I see when I smell the coppery tang my own blood. When my ragged breaths come in excruciating gulps, each one more labored than the last.

In these final fading moments, I expect my life's memories to unspool like an old film reel, a kaleidoscope of vibrant colors and sounds highlighting my journey's most poignant scenes. But instead? All I can see is what never happened.

The extravagant and grandiose event that was supposed to be the highlight of my life. Instead of a fulfilling and colorful existence... all I see is white.

Including the little white lie that brought on my death.

PART 1

REESE

CHAPTER ONE

It's a funny way to meet your future fiancé—at the cake tasting for his wedding to another woman—but that is exactly how Tucker and I met.

Let me clarify, I'm not some bridal bouquet-chasing bachelorette stalking cake tastings for a husband. It's quite the opposite, actually. I'm the proud owner of Couture Cakes, a charming little bakery nestled in the historic town of Somerville, South Carolina. And, up until a year ago, I was perfectly happy being single and dating around while growing my buttercream empire.

That is until the "couple of the moment" walked into my shop.

The upcoming nuptials of Tucker Harding and Charlotte Spencer were poised to be the stuff of Southern legend. Charlotte, the epitome of a born-and-bred Southern belle, hailed from a family tree dripping with old money—the kind of wealth that probably had roots tangled up in the plantation era. Their fortunes might have taken a few hits over the years, but they were likely still at the top of Southern society.

Charlotte herself was a walking, talking advertisement for the privileges of generational affluence. She had soft platinum locks, piercing sapphire eyes, and meticulously manicured, well, *everything*. She exuded the effortless confidence of someone who'd never had to lift a finger in her life. The world was her oyster, and she knew it.

Tucker was an entirely different story. Tall and devastatingly handsome, but with dark eyes and hair, like a villain from one of those vampire shows. His inky black waves, smoldering espresso eyes, and square jawline were enough to make even the most jaded spinster do a double take. In addition, Tucker was adopted from India as a child, adding a layer of complexity to his charm.

But he had more going for him than just good looks—Tucker had earned his place among the Southern elite. As the mastermind behind his own wildly successful import-export empire, he'd built a fortune that rivaled even the most storied of family names. And if the rumors were true, he was the one bankrolling this lavish affair.

So, when I received a call that they were interested in having me design the cake for their wedding? I was practically beside myself with excitement.

Bernadette, whom I affectionately call Bernie, and I had been meticulously planning for this tasting for weeks, obsessing over every detail to ensure perfection. When the day of the tasting arrived and the couple finally arrived at my door, they were exactly as I had envisioned in my mind's eye. Charlotte looked poised and polished in a fitted white pantsuit that probably cost as much as my stand mixer. Meanwhile, Tucker looked equally dashing in a navy sport coat.

I immediately felt self-conscious in their presence,

brushing back a lock of my pin-straight red hair and smoothing my pale pink apron. In fact, rumor had it they'd snagged the most coveted venue in the South—Magnolia, a historic plantation that commanded a five-figure price tag just to book the space. For a small-town baker like me, landing this gig would be a game changer.

Let's be honest, it wasn't *just* about the prestige. I needed that wedding like I needed air in my lungs. The once-shiny veneer of my little shop was starting to crack under the weight of mounting expenses. That secondhand oven I'd been coaxing along for years? It was on its last legs, threatening to give out at any moment. Sure, we had a lot of work, but it was mostly just your middle-class, run-of-the-mill client who spent a few hundred bucks on their wedding cake. Not enough to glean much of a profit margin. I was running on fumes, desperately trying to keep up with the demand while my meager crew of two stretched ourselves to the breaking point.

Charlotte took the lead when they arrived, gliding forward with an outstretched hand and a dazzling smile.

"Reese, darling, it's an absolute pleasure to finally meet you in person," she gushed, her perfectly manicured fingers wrapping around mine in a grip that was both delicate and viselike.

"Likewise, Miss Spencer," I replied.

As she brushed past me and headed to the tasting table, I found my gaze drifting toward Tucker. He stood just behind his fiancée, with a quiet intensity that seemed to fill the room. When he stepped forward to shake my hand, I felt an electric jolt run up my arm, sending a shiver of something forbidden down my spine.

"Reese, it's nice to meet you. Your bakery is lovely," he

said. I believe I mumbled something akin to *thank you* in return. Honestly, it was hard not to gape at how gorgeous he was.

Get it together, Reese. He's engaged, I thought, trying to push the inappropriate thoughts aside. I couldn't help but feel a twinge of envy as I watched Charlotte loop her arm possessively through Tucker's.

I pasted on my most professional smile and ushered the couple toward the table, determined to focus on the task at hand. I had to nail this tasting, to prove to Charlotte and Tucker—and perhaps, to myself—that I was the right choice for their big day.

When Charlotte sat down at the table, her eyes sparkled with delight. "Oh my goodness, Reese! This place is an absolute dream," she gushed, her voice dripping with honeyed charm. I followed her gaze around the room as she took in every lovingly curated detail—the vintage white cupboard bursting with colorful teacups and dishes, the soft pink taffeta curtains that billowed gently in the breeze from the large picture window.

I felt a swell of pride in my chest, but it was quickly tempered by a nagging voice in the back of my mind. *Will it be enough?*

"Thank you so much, Miss Spencer," I replied, my voice steady despite the butterflies in my stomach. "I've poured my heart and soul into every inch of this place. It means the world to hear you say that."

Charlotte turned to me, her perfectly manicured hand resting on her hip. "Please, call me Charlotte. We're practically family now, aren't we?" She winked conspiratorially. I felt a blush creep up my neck.

"Of course, Charlotte," I said. To be honest? I thought it

was a little over the top. But I was willing to play along. "I'm thrilled to have you and Tucker here today. I've prepared a special selection of cakes for you to sample, each one a labor of love."

I launched into my carefully rehearsed spiel about the cakes I'd prepared. Everything was going to plan, but I couldn't quite shake the buzzy feeling I had when Tucker's eyes would linger on me for a second too long.

Just as we settled in to take our first bites of the prepared confections, the silver bell above the front door chimed. In glided an elderly woman, her hair so blonde it was almost white, and eyes the same piercing crystal blue as Charlotte's. It was clear that the mother of the bride had arrived.

Charlotte immediately sprang up from her seat and knocked back her chair. Tucker stood up from his seat to help, but she quickly recovered, setting the chair upright before rushing to escort her mother to our table. "I hope you don't mind, but I took the liberty of inviting my mother to join us today," she announced, her voice a bit shaky. Her cheeks were bright pink.

I caught the fleeting look of annoyance that flickered across Tucker's face, but he quickly smoothed it over with a practiced smile.

Interesting, I remember thinking. *Trouble in paradise, perhaps?*

"Of course," I said aloud, my own smile never wavering. "I'll have another place setting prepared immediately." I spun on my heel and made a beeline for the back of the shop, calling out to Bernie to get another table setting ready.

When I returned to the table a few moments later, the atmosphere had shifted palpably. Charlotte, previously the picture of poise, was now fidgeting nervously, her perfectly polished nails picking at the delicate skin around her cuticles. Mrs. Spencer, on the other hand, wore a placid expression that seemed almost too serene, like the calm before a storm. And Tucker? His earlier irritation had morphed into something darker, a restless energy that made him shift in his seat like a caged animal.

"So," I began, my voice cutting through the tension like a knife through butter, "what did you have in mind for the cake?"

The rest of the meeting passed in a whirlwind of details —the towering tiers, the groom's cake, the endless sea of cupcakes for the after-party. But looking back, it's not the specifics of the order that stand out in my memory. It's the tension between the three of them—the way Tucker rolled his eyes when no one was looking, or how the bride's mother interrupted her daughter or answered my questions before Charlotte could get a word out.

In the end, I landed the job. I had just over a month to prepare for the wedding of the year. I couldn't deny I was growing more fond of Tucker, who came back to the shop a handful of times before the big wedding. He would often stop by just to chat or fulfill a craving for one of my chocolate beignets. Once, he even pulled me away for a coffee break, where we chatted for an hour over lattes. These little moments, no matter how brief, had become the highlight of my day.

So, when the fateful call came on the day of the Spencer-Harding wedding, informing me that the nuptials had been abruptly canceled, I'm ashamed to admit that a small, selfish part of me rejoiced. I couldn't deny I was attracted Tucker, and I thought he might feel the same way.

I repeatedly offered to refund him for the cost of the

wedding cake, but he refused. He did stop by the shop for several weeks after, feigning a craving for one of my famous cupcakes. About a month later, he asked me out to dinner, an invite I gladly accepted.

Now here we are, a year later.

And in just five days, I'll be the one walking down the aisle to meet Tucker at the altar. His new blushing bride.

CHAPTER TWO

FIVE DAYS BEFORE THE WEDDING

"Reese," I hear a voice call out from the back of the bakery. "The walk-in cooler is down again. Do you want me to call the repair man?"

"Of course it is," I mumble quietly, even though no one can hear me. I'm halfway through restocking the front display case, my hand frozen in the air over a delightful strawberry cupcake. The cooler has been on the fritz for months, adding to the list of items that need repaired, or worse, replaced. My previously lighthearted mood instantly turns dark. *I swear I spend more time on hold with contractors than I do actually baking.*

It's been nearly two years since I first laid eyes on my little space on Main Street. It still has charm—the quaint scalloped awning, the oversized picture window, the vintage limestone façade—and all the same problems. I often wonder how Mr. and Mrs. Romano, the sweet old couple who leased the space before me, managed to keep things afloat for nearly two decades. They still drop in from time to time, and we've become friends. Somerville is a small community, and I was met with some resistance when they relinquished the space to me and I began to transform it into what it is now. But eventually I won everyone over with my irresistible cupcakes and, the staple of the South, beignets.

I glance at the photo hanging behind the register—a younger me, flour-dusted and grinning, baking alongside Grandma Mae in her cozy kitchen. It's my morning ritual to press my fingers to my lips and then gently touch the frame. "Morning, Grandma Mae," I whisper, a soft smile playing on my lips.

She taught me everything I know about baking, and the small inheritance she left me allowed me to open up this bakery in the first place. I pour my heart into every creation, hoping that her legacy will live on through my shop. On days like today—when another piece of equipment fails me—her memory is about the only thing that keeps me going.

Wedding cakes, in particular, require an unparalleled level of precision and attention to detail. Every sugar flower must be expertly crafted, and every swipe of frosting a perfect shade of ivory. With anxious brides and their mothers scrutinizing every move, the pressure to deliver flawless results is immense. One tiny mistake could tarnish my reputation and send the entire business crumbling down.

Over the last two years since I opened the shop, I've been taking some of our profits, which were fairly slim in the beginning, and reinvesting them back into the building. The HVAC was something that needed a complete replacement.

Tucker has offered to help, of course. More times than I can count, he's gently suggested that he could cover the cost of the new system, that it would be a small thing for him to do. And every time, I've politely but firmly declined. It's not about pride, exactly. It's more about proving to myself that I can do this, that I have what it takes to build something lasting and real, without relying on someone else to swoop in and save the day.

I know he means well. He's seen firsthand how hard I've worked, how much of myself I've poured into this little shop. But accepting his help feels like admitting defeat, like conceding that maybe I'm not cut out for this after all. And that's a thought I just can't bear.

"No." I brush a bit of hair back over my ear. "I'll call them, Bernie. Thanks for letting me know."

Bernie emerges from the back of the bakery. She's a few years younger than me, with a work ethic that rivals my own. She's got these expressive brown eyes that always seem to be laughing at some private joke, and a mop of dark brown hair that she usually keeps tied back in a no-nonsense ponytail.

Right now, she's wearing a slight frown on her face. I know her well enough to know she has some not-so-great news.

"I hate to add to your plate, but we just got a last-minute cookie order for a baby shower. They need five dozen decorated sugar cookies by tomorrow afternoon."

My shoulders sag, the burden of yet another task settling heavily upon me.

"Tomorrow?" I ask, my mind already churning with the logistics of fitting this order into our already packed schedule. "That's cutting it a bit close, isn't it?"

Bernie nods, her expression sympathetic. "I know, but when I tried to explain the tight schedule, she said she would pay a rush fee. She sounded desperate."

"Alright," I say, my resolve hardening. "Prep the cookies, and I'll come back and finish them up after we close up the shop."

Bernie frowns, concern etching lines into her forehead. "Reese, I'm sorry. I know you're burning the candle at both ends."

I wave off her concern, forcing a smile that feels brittle around the edges. "I'm fine, Bernie. Really. This is just a busy season, that's all. Once we get through the gala and the wedding, things will settle down."

But even as the words leave my mouth, I know they ring hollow. The truth is, I can't remember the last time I felt truly rested, truly at peace. It's like I'm always running, always chasing after the next big order or the next glowing review, never quite able to catch my breath. It doesn't help that my fiancé is a workaholic as well. Sometimes I wonder if we'll ever have time to even start a family.

Bernie straightens. "I'll get started right away."

Thank goodness for Bernie, I think as she heads back to the kitchen. When I first hired her, I wasn't sure what to expect. I've always been a bit of a lone wolf, preferring to handle things on my own rather than relying on others. But Bernie has a way of growing on you, of making herself indispensable before you even realize what's happening.

Honestly, I don't know what I'd do without her.

With a sigh, I weave my way back to the glorified broom closet I call an office, tucked away in the far corner of the shop. I've managed to cram a tiny desk, a filing cabinet, and a couple of shelves into the small room, creating a space Bernie has generously described as "cozy."

Just as I'm reaching for the phone to call the repairman, the familiar chime of the front doorbell echoes through the shop. I hesitate for a moment, my hand hovering over the receiver. Part of me is hoping it's just the UPS driver making a routine delivery. With our regular orders, the gala, and the wedding consuming every waking moment, I'm not sure I have the capacity to take on even one more order this week. Especially now with the baby shower cookies.

I take a deep breath, square my shoulders, and make my way to the front of the shop. But as soon as I lay eyes on the person gracing the threshold, my heart plummets—it's literally the *last* person I want to see.

CHAPTER THREE

"Good morning, Reese," says the man standing before me, his Southern drawl as smooth as butter.

"Zach," I reply, my heart doing a tap dance in my chest. "What are you doing here? I thought we agreed not to meet at the shop?"

Zach is my main point of contact for the museum gala reception.

He's also my ex-boyfriend.

While my fiancé is all exotic charm and mystery, Zach is the quintessential Southern gentleman. His soft brown hair, sun-kissed in the summer, perfectly complements his baby-blue eyes and clean-shaven face. He's the kind of guy who wears pale blue seersucker jackets and fitted jeans with leather loafers, making all the Southern belles swoon. And yes, I'll admit, there was a time when I fell for his charms too. *Hard.*

But that was before I met Tucker.

"I thought we could grab a coffee and discuss the upcoming event this Saturday," he says, his eyes twinkling with a hint of mischief. He *knows* we're not supposed to meet at the shop. Tucker frequently drops in to check on me and if he found Zach here, he'd be furious. Not that he has anything to worry about. But some men tend to be more territorial and Tucker just happens to be one of those.

I shake my head dramatically, a strand of my unruly red hair breaking loose.

"Oh, you mean my wedding?"

"Come on, Reese." Zach rolls his eyes. "The gala?"

It's ironic, given that a gala is exactly how Zach and I met. I was there, showcasing my desserts, when he sauntered over and struck up a conversation. We quickly discovered that we had more in common than just a sweet tooth—we both loved the arts. We were hot and heavy for all of six months, before Tucker walked into my shop and changed everything.

I purse my lips. "I have a wedding as well. And you know it. Which is why I told you not to drop by here."

"I'm well aware," he says, his shoulders falling slightly.

I feel a tightness seize my chest. It's still there, the *guilt*. The way I broke up with Zach, well, it wasn't exactly fair. There were a couple of weeks where I was seeing both him and Tucker, torn between the two of them. But in the end, Tucker was the one I knew I'd marry.

I broke up with Zach right after he caught Tucker and me having dinner together. He's never quite recovered from the blow.

"Now, what did you want to discuss?" I ask.

"The macarons. I had some ideas for how to incorporate the colors with the rest of the artwork on display."

I let out a frustrated sigh. Bernie and I were supposed to start on those macarons first thing tomorrow morning. I guess

I have no choice but to meet with Zach now, otherwise it will throw off our entire schedule.

"What kind of ideas?"

"Well, Mrs. Carrington has donated a rare natural black pearl necklace that's worth a small fortune. We'll be auctioning it off during the event. I'd like to give it more attention by creating some coordinating desserts that match the color."

"A black pearl?"

He shakes his head slightly. "It's not actually black. Listen, how about we head to Marla's for coffee. I have some photos I want to show you."

I look into Zach's blue eyes, taking in his earnest expression. I truly have no idea what a natural black pearl looks like, so he's got me there. But let's be honest, this isn't *just* about the macarons. The wedding is just a few days away, and Zach has been popping in more frequently these last few weeks. His words from our last conversation echo in my mind.

"Reese, I know it's not my place, but I can't watch you make this mistake without saying something," he had said, his voice filled with concern. "Tucker isn't right for you. Remember how you told me he stood you up last week because he got called off to Tokyo? He's always putting his business before you. Is that really the kind of man you want to spend the rest of your life with?"

His doubts had struck a chord within me, and now, as I stand before him, I can't help but second-guess my decision. *What if Zach is right? What if Tucker isn't the one?*

I shake my head. It's too late for doubts now, especially with so much left to do for the wedding preparations. I can't let Zach's words sway me, not when I've already committed to Tucker.

Either way, we have a gala to prepare for. And apparently some black pearl necklace needs to get its due attention. "Fine. Give me a few minutes."

I flag down Bernie and tell her I'll be stepping out for a bit. I grab my purse and catch a glimpse of myself in the mirror. My pale, freckled skin is clear, but my blue eyes look dull. With a quick motion, I pluck a stray strand of red hair and attempt to smooth it into place. I let out a sigh. Let's face it, I look every bit the part of a stressed-out bride-to-be.

As Zach pulls open the front door for me, I feel a small tug of guilt. I probably shouldn't be having coffee with my ex, given our history. But Zach came to me with an offer I couldn't refuse—a chance to cater the desserts for a swanky cocktail reception at the Charleston Museum. It is a dream come true for Couture Cakes. The exposure alone will be worth it.

The event is the museum's annual "Art of Giving" gala, a glittering affair that brings together the city's most influential philanthropists and art enthusiasts for an evening of charity and culture. The highlight of the night is always the grand auction, where one-of-a-kind pieces are sold to the highest bidder, with all proceeds going to support the museum's outreach programs for underprivileged children.

This year's theme is *Under the Sea,* and the event organizers have spared no expense to wow donors and guests. Apparently there will even be a live mermaid swimming in a giant tank in the center of the room. I rolled my eyes when Zach told me.

Only in the South.

Aside from the over-the-top presentation, it is for a fabulous cause, and it's a great way for Couture Cakes to make an impact in the community. So, when Zach approached me about being a part of the gala, I jumped at the chance.

I threw myself into the preparations, pouring all of my creativity and expertise into crafting a menu that would fit in with the over-the-top theme. I spent weeks experimenting with flavors and textures, dreaming up miniature works of food art. There are dainty shell-shaped tartlets topped with delicate sprigs of candied red coral, dark chocolate truffles infused with bourbon, and airy macarons in a rainbow of under-the-sea tones.

But the real showstopper is the centerpiece I designed especially for the event—a towering croquembouche accented with candied pearls and shimmering coral. It's a French pastry I saw at a food expo in Charleston once, and I've been dying to make one ever since. The one I've created is made up of dozens of delicate cream puffs, all painstakingly wrapped in caramel and stacked into a gravity-defying cone. While it isn't enough of a spectacle to compete with a live mermaid, it should be enough to wow the guests.

The only problem? Tucker would blow a gasket if he found out I was working with Zach. So, I may have excluded that little detail when I told him about the gala. I mentioned that Couture Cakes was catering, but I conveniently left out the fact that Zach was my primary contact for the event. A little detail that may well get me into trouble.

CHAPTER FOUR

Ten minutes later, Zach and I are seated at Marla's, which used to be a favorite spot of ours. Just like my shop, it has an eclectic feel, with a collection of mismatched furniture, local artwork, and homemade goods. The café is nearly always busy, locals and tourists filling the room with a gentle buzz of conversation. It's exactly what you'd expect in a small Southern town.

Zach approaches the counter and orders our usual lattes. I watch him from the table, chewing the inside of my cheek. Even after our breakup, he was adamant that we stay friends. Zach would never speak about his exes, even though I know he dated someone pretty seriously before me, so I wasn't sure how he would act after our split. I was a little surprised he wanted to stay friends at first, since he basically caught me cheating on him, but given I'm a transplant here in the South and don't have many friends, I reluctantly agreed.

After we spend a few minutes discussing the black pearl —which is actually more of an iridescent blue—and how we can work it into the macarons, Zach turns the conversation toward the wedding.

"So, how are you holding up?" he asks, his blue eyes filled with concern. As soon as he mentions it, I glance warily toward the front door. I half expect Tucker to come strolling in at any moment, catching me red-handed. Of course, I have a good explanation as to why I'm meeting with Zach, but I'm not sure Tucker would understand why the discussion of a black pearl would warrant the two of us sitting down for coffee.

And he would be right.

I pull my attention back to Zach, who is silently waiting for my answer, and let out a long sigh.

"Honestly? I now understand why brides come into my shop looking like they've been through a war. And I've only been at this for a month. The pressure is unreal, even *with* a wedding planner. I don't know ninety-five percent of the people coming, but I feel like I've sold my soul to make them all happy."

Zach chuckles and takes a sip of his coffee. "Welcome to the South, Reese. Down here, making everyone else happy while looking picture-perfect is an art form."

Perhaps Zach and I have different ideas about what can be considered art. But even as he speaks, I can't help but think about how *fast* everything's happened. One month from proposal to 'I do'? It's like I'm frosting a wedding cake before the layers have even cooled. A tiny voice in my head wonders if we should've given it more time, but I quickly push those thoughts aside.

I *know* Tucker is the one.

"I'm starting to see why Charlotte didn't go through with her wedding," I say, trying to make light of the situation.

"The idea of being a runaway bride is becoming more appealing by the minute."

The clatter of porcelain plates and coffee cups fills the background as Zach leans in, his voice lowering to a conspiratorial whisper. "Do you ever wonder why she ran away?"

I raise an eyebrow. "What do you mean?"

"Think about it, Reese. She vanished into thin air on her wedding day, and no one has seen or heard from her since, aside from a few social media posts. Don't you find that a bit...peculiar?"

Of course I find it odd. But I try not to dwell on Charlotte. She's Tucker's ex, and their failed relationship has nothing to do with me. At least, that's what I keep telling myself.

The truth is, I've thought about Charlotte a lot over the past year. It's hard not to, when the shadow of her disappearance seems to loom over everything. I've caught myself wondering what could have happened to her, why she would have walked away from her life without so much as a word to anyone.

Charlotte obviously comes from a well-to-do family, one that would have the resources to find her if she was actually missing. Her mother Amanda, whom I only met the one time at my shop, has hardly been seen or heard from either. She maintains that her daughter left and doesn't wish to be contacted. I only hear bits and pieces from the patrons at the shop, and I try to appear as uninterested as possible. Even though I'm carefully listening for any morsel of information as to why she left.

Of course, Tucker is the one person who must know what happened. But I learned quickly that Charlotte is a sore subject with him. Whenever her name comes up, I can see the pain and anger that flash in his eyes, the way his jaw clenches and his whole body seems to tense. I know that their breakup was messy, that there are wounds there that haven't quite healed. So I never bring her up, never probe too deeply into the mystery of her vanishing act. I figure that if Tucker wants to talk about it, he will. And if not, well, that's his business.

But now, with Zach's words echoing in my mind, I find myself feeling slightly uneasy. He's right, after all. Charlotte's disappearance is more than just peculiar—it's downright bizarre.

"I guess," I finally say.

"She up and left, right before the wedding," Zach continues, his eyes narrowing. "What could have possibly happened between her and Tucker that would cause her to run away?"

I nod my head, feeling the all-too-familiar tension in my back creeping up to my neck. In an attempt to ease the discomfort, I press my fingertips against my shoulder. But the thought that something sinister may have occurred—involving my future husband—lingers in my mind, adding to the stress already weighing me down. As if planning a wedding wasn't enough of a burden, I've got to deal with everyone's questions about Charlotte as well.

"It's in the past, Zach," I say, giving up on the tension in my shoulders and tipping back the last of my coffee. "Listen, I need to get back to the shop and then head over to the Charleston Place Hotel for the party Monica's having for me."

Zach's eyebrows shoot up, and a smirk plays on his lips. "Ah, yes. The infamous bridal luncheon. Sounds like a lamb being served up to a den of hungry lions."

I can't help but chuckle at his analogy. Monica Harding, Tucker's cousin, is known for her sharp tongue and ability to make even the most confident person feel like they're under a microscope. I've only met her once, and honestly, once was enough. But she's going to be my cousin by marriage soon, so I guess I have to get used to her.

"You're not wrong," I say. "But trust me, I can handle myself."

I'm trying to appear confident, but the truth is I am dreading this luncheon. Give me a scorching oven and a mixer any day—I can whip up a three-tier masterpiece without breaking a sweat. But put me in a room full of Botox-laden Southern belles armed with their razor-sharp tongues and judgmental glares?

I'd rather face a firing squad.

"Just be careful, Reese. Those society ladies can smell fear," Zach teases, his blue eyes filled with mirth.

"I'll keep that in mind," I say, rolling my eyes playfully. One of the things I've always enjoyed about Zach is our playful banter. I can't name a time when he didn't make me laugh. "Now, I really must go. I'll incorporate your ideas for the macarons, and you can work out the details with Bernadette before Saturday."

"Of course." He nods, his smile fading a bit. "I'll touch base with Bernie and sort everything out."

I stand to leave, when Zach reaches out and traces a finger down the back of my hand. The unexpected touch sends a shiver through me, and I instinctively glance toward the door, half-expecting Tucker to walk in and catch us in the moment.

"Remember, if you need a break from the lions, you know where to find me," he says.

I meet his gaze, searching for any hint of ulterior motives behind his offer of friendship. Is he genuinely concerned about my well-being, or is this just another attempt to drive a wedge between Tucker and me? The guilt of our past affair weighs heavily on my shoulders, and I can't help but wonder if Zach's intentions are as pure as he claims.

"Thanks, Zach. I'll keep that in mind," I reply, my voice wavering slightly as I pull my hand away from his touch.

As I make my way to the door, I feel off-balance, my mind reeling with conflicting emotions. The wedding preparations have been stressful enough without the added complication of Zach's presence in my life, not to mention the ghost of Charlotte looming over me like a dark cloud. But, when the warm sunlight hits my skin, I breathe in deeply, the faint smell of honeysuckle filling my nostrils. Regardless of what happened before, I have a wedding to plan, a bridal luncheon to attend, and a future to look forward to with Tucker.

The past is in the past. *For now.*

CHAPTER FIVE

The Charleston Place Hotel has been a fixture of Charleston's landscape for over a century, a symbol of the city's grandeur and elegance. The hotel first opened its doors in 1853, then managed to survive the devastation of the Civil War and the economic upheaval that followed. Over the years, the hotel has played host to a who's who of American history. Presidents have slept in its suites, literary giants have penned masterpieces in its writing rooms, and Hollywood starlets have graced its ballrooms with their presence.

And now, here I am, a small-town baker from Tennessee wearing a designer dress I rented online and a set of pearl earrings I borrowed from Mrs. Romano. Tucker surprised me last week with a pale pink Chanel bag, which I am now clutching to my chest like a piece of armor. I feel about as out of place here as a weed in a bed of prizewinning roses.

It takes me a few minutes to navigate through the storied halls, but eventually I find my way to the private room where the bridal luncheon is being held. I open the doors and step inside.

It comes as no surprise that Monica has gone all out to decorate the room for the party. Every table is adorned with white linens and an abundant display of freshly cut white roses, pink peonies, and fragrant lilies. There's a giant wall of flowers in the corner of the room for guests to snap a photo for their socials, and the place settings are full of delicate crystal and polished silver, carefully wrapped napkins with matching ribbons.

I immediately start to scan the room for a familiar face. There are about thirty women present and Monica is the only person I know.

Zach was right. *I'm truly a lamb being fed to the lions.*

"Reese, darling!" Monica trills, and she zigzags toward me from across the room. She's wearing a fitted lace sundress that hugs her curves in all the right places, radiating an air of effortless elegance. Her raven hair is set in loose waves that frame her striking emerald eyes.

She grabs my shoulders and begins to air-kiss my cheeks with the precision of a surgeon. "I'm so thrilled you could make it. Come, let me introduce you to the girls."

Tucker's cousin is the epitome of Southern charm, all perfectly coiffed hair and impeccable manners. But beneath that sugary exterior is a core of steel. She is the undisputed queen bee of Charleston society, and the kind of woman who can make or break a reputation with a single raised eyebrow. I've heard stories about Monica from the patrons of my shop, whispered gossip that paints her as a force to be reckoned with.

As she leads me through the crowd of chattering women, a flutter of nervousness stirs in my stomach. Every move I make, every word I speak, will be scrutinized and judged. And this isn't just about impressing them at fancy events, it's

about securing my place beside Tucker in the upper eche-
lons of society. One misstep and my dreams of a perfect life
with him will crumble to dust.

I allow myself to be swept into the whirlwind of intro-
ductions, trying desperately to keep track of the endless
stream of double-barreled names and designer labels. There's
Shelby Ann, the former beauty queen with a laugh like a
hyena on helium; Caroline Louise, the trust fund baby with a
penchant for polo players; and Eliza Jane, the aspiring Insta-
gram influencer who seems to have a filter for every occasion.

As we settle onto the plush upholstered furniture, a veri-
table army of servers descends upon us, bearing trays of
dainty finger sandwiches and miniature quiches. I nibble on
a cucumber round, trying to ignore the fact that it probably
costs more than my entire weekly grocery budget.

After a few rounds of mimosas, the conversation begins
to flow freely, with topics ranging from the latest charity gala
to the newest Botox injector in town. Caroline Louise settles
down into a chair opposite mine.

"Reese, darling," she purrs, her eyes glinting with a
mischievous light. "I couldn't help but overhear that you're
working with Zach Caldwell on the museum gala. He's quite
the catch, isn't he?"

My cheeks flush, a telltale sign of discomfort that I'm
sure isn't lost on Caroline. "Oh, well, yes, Zach and I are
collaborating on the dessert menu," I stammer, trying to keep
my tone light and breezy. "But it's strictly professional."

She arches a delicately sculpted eyebrow, a smirk playing
at the corners of her lips. "Really? Because I seem to
remember hearing rumors that you two were quite the item
back in the day. Something about a steamy encounter at a
gallery opening?"

I nearly choke on my mimosa, my eyes widening in horror. I can feel the heat rising in my cheeks. "That...was a long time ago," I manage to sputter.

Caroline leans in closer, her voice dropping to a whisper. "Don't worry, darling, your secret is safe with me. But I have to wonder...what does Tucker think about you working so closely with an ex-flame? Especially one as dashing as Zach?"

I glance around the room, desperate for an escape route, but all I see are curious eyes and barely concealed smirks. And there, in the corner, I catch sight of Monica. She is chatting with another woman, but keeping one eye trained on the two of us.

Now I'm in trouble. One word of this to Tucker and I'll have a whole new set of problems to deal with.

I take a deep breath, forcing myself to meet her gaze head-on. "Tucker is fully supportive of my work with the museum," I say, my voice steady and unwavering. "He knows that Zach and I are just colleagues, nothing more. And he trusts me completely."

Caroline's smirk only widens, her eyes dancing with barely contained glee. She leans back and waves her hand. "Of course he does, darling. But you know how men can be. So possessive, so easily threatened. I just hope you know what you're doing, mixing business with pleasure like that."

A surge of anger rises up in my chest, hot and fierce. How dare she insinuate that I would ever betray Tucker's trust, that I would risk everything we've built together for some silly flirtation?

But before I can open my mouth to deliver a scathing retort, Monica swoops in. "Caroline, darling, I've been meaning to ask you about that new brow lift of yours. Who did you go to, and how much did it set you back?"

Caroline's eyes widen, her hand flying up to her forehead. "I...I don't know what you're talking about," she stammers, her voice suddenly uncertain.

But Monica just laughs, a tinkling sound that seems to cut through the tension like a knife. "Oh, don't be coy, darling. We're all friends here."

"Oh, well, it was Dr. Stevens," she stutters. "He—"

"Right. Dr. Stevens," Monica replies, cutting her off mid-sentence. She then turns to me, her smile softening into something almost genuine. "Anyway, Reese, darling, why don't you come with me? I have some people I'd love for you to meet."

I nod gratefully, allowing myself to be led away from Caroline's piercing gaze. Monica gives me a sideways glance and I mouth the words *thank you*.

Honestly, Monica was the last person I expected to come to my aid. Our interactions have always been a delicate dance, each word carefully chosen, each reaction scrutinized. She's never given me the impression that she particularly likes or dislikes me, always maintaining a polite but distant demeanor. But today, she stepped in when I needed someone most, and I feel a tiny glimmer of hope.

Perhaps there's more to Monica than I've given her credit for. Maybe, just maybe, she likes me after all.

CHAPTER SIX

After almost two hours of idle chatter and nibbling on hors d'oeuvres, my jaw is starting to ache from the forced smile that I'm wearing. Everything has been going smoothly so far, aside from the awkward conversation about Zach and the museum gala. As the drinks and snacks start to dwindle, I mentally begin plotting my escape. I only took a few sips of my mimosa before switching to coffee, knowing I need to return to the shop to finish the baby shower cookies before meeting Tucker at home.

Just as I'm about to make my move, the conversation turns to the one topic everyone is avoiding but surely thinking about—Charlotte, the missing ex-fiancée.

"I always knew that girl was trouble," Shelby Ann declares, her eyebrows knitting together in disapproval. "She was just too perfect, you know? Like, who actually volunteers at the animal shelter and teaches Sunday school?"

Caroline nods, taking a delicate sip of her mimosa. "Imagine how her mother must feel. I've heard she barely leaves the house now. That she's practically a recluse."

"Poor Mrs. Spencer," says Shelby Ann, tilting her head sympathetically. "First she loses her husband and then her only daughter leaves town without a word."

"Where do you think she went?" I ask quietly.

"A fabulous beach somewhere in the Caribbean is my guess," says Eliza Jane. "Didn't you see that post she put on social media? A picture of a mai tai with the ocean in the background. She captioned it 'I'm fine, everyone. Stop messaging me.'"

Shelby Ann nods. "Yeah, I saw it. It makes sense that she'd be on a beach, because I heard she ran away with one of those charter boat captains." Then she shrugs. "But no one knows for sure."

I shift uncomfortably in my seat, suddenly feeling trapped as the conversation turns to Charlotte's disappearance. It's clear that her absence has left a gaping hole in this tight-knit circle of friends, but the reactions around the table are as varied as the women themselves.

Caroline looks visibly distressed. "I just don't understand," she says, her voice trembling. "Charlotte never mentioned anything about having doubts or second thoughts. And now, she's gone without a word. Not even a single text to let me know she's okay."

The hurt and confusion in her eyes is palpable, and I find myself feeling a pang of sympathy for her.

"Didn't you get the Christmas card? Charlotte may have left without a word, but she still managed to send out holiday cards this year. One of those gold-embellished numbers from that expensive shop she uses in New York."

"Yes, I did, but..."

As the discussion continues, I notice the mixed emotions swirling around the table. Some of the women seem genuinely concerned for Charlotte's well-being, while others appear indifferent, as if her disappearance is nothing more than a momentary distraction from their own lives.

I can only imagine how many of these women stood beside Charlotte on their own wedding days, giggling and sipping champagne as she helped adjust their veil or touch up their lipstick. They probably shared countless secrets and inside jokes, forging the kind of bonds that only come from years of friendship. And then, without warning, Charlotte was gone. No goodbye, no explanation, just a void where a vibrant presence once stood.

But just when I start to feel empathy for them, Eliza Jane leans in, her eyes gleaming with mischief. "Speaking of Charlotte," she stage-whispers, "I heard she and Tucker had quite the, ahem, active sex life. Apparently, she had a thing for role-playing. You know, like nurse and patient, cop and robber, that sort of thing."

I nearly choke on my coffee, my face suddenly burning red. *Is she serious right now?*

Shelby Ann turns to me, a wicked gleam in her eye. "What about you, Reese? Has Tucker ever mentioned any of his kinky little secrets? I mean, you're about to marry the man. Surely you must know all about his dirty laundry."

I can't believe she has the nerve to ask me that. Maybe Charlotte was right to leave. *These women are savage.*

I open my mouth to respond, but all that comes out is an embarrassing squeak. The answer is no, Tucker is not into kinky role-play, but I'm not about to dish the dirt on our sex life. Just as I am about to make an excuse to leave, Monica appears and claps her hands together.

"Ladies!" she chirps. "It's time for the cake pull!"

I breathe a sigh of relief. *Finally*. Once the cake pull is over, I'm free to make a quick exit.

For those not in the know, a cake pull is a long-standing Southern tradition where charms are baked into the wedding cake, each one symbolizing a different blessing for the bride and her attendants. It's supposed to be a sweet, lighthearted moment, a chance to celebrate the future. But honestly, I feel like the whole thing is a bit childish. The idea that a tiny trinket baked into a cake could somehow predict or shape our futures seems more than a little far-fetched to me. I mean, really? A miniature horseshoe is going to magically bring me good fortune and success? *Please*.

The double doors of the event room swing open, and a uniformed waiter pushes a cart into the room, bearing a stunning three-tiered white cake. The baker in me can't help but analyze the design, and I have to admit, I'm impressed. The cake is a masterpiece of sugared roses and expertly airbrushed stencils. It sits atop a large silver platter, with about two dozen cords dangling over the side, each one tied to a handwritten name card.

One by one, the ladies take their turn, each one retrieving a unique charm with its own special meaning. There's a heart for true love, a key for new opportunities, and a four-leaf clover for good luck. Each charm is met with gasps of delight and excited chatter.

"Look, look, it's a baby rattle!" gasps Shelby Anne.

"Oh, you know what that means," Caroline chimes in. "Time to start picking out colors for the nursery!"

As I watch the spectacle unfold, I resist the urge to roll my eyes. *Are these ladies for real?* But as I glance around at the faces of the women surrounding me, I realize that my skepticism is decidedly in the minority. They're all buying into this wholeheartedly, *ooh*ing and *ahh*ing over each charm like it's a priceless treasure.

I suppose I shouldn't be surprised. After all, the South is steeped in traditions and superstitions, from burying bourbon bottles to ward off rain on wedding days to never taking a new broom when you move lest you sweep away your good luck. And if I'm being honest, that old-fashioned charm is part of what drew me to this place to begin with.

Still, as I watch Vivienne practically swoon over her champagne flute charm and Genevieve wax poetic about the deep symbolism of her butterfly, I can't quite suppress the wry smile that tugs at the corners of my mouth. It all just seems so...silly. Like we're a bunch of grown women playing at being little girls, pinning our hopes and dreams on bits of metal and enamel.

Then again, who am I to judge? I bake fairy-tale-style wedding cakes for a living.

Suddenly it's my turn. I step up to the cake, my heart fluttering with nervous excitement as I reach for the name card with Reese neatly written across it. I give the cord a gentle tug, feeling the resistance as the charm emerges from the depths of the cake.

When I hold it up to the light, my breath catches in my chest. There, dangling from the end of the ribbon, is a tiny silver knife, its blade glinting menacingly in the soft glow of the chandeliers. At the tip of the knife is a tiny bit of painted-on blood.

A bloody knife? My mind reels. What is a bloody knife supposed to represent? It can't be anything good. If my memory serves me, in the language of cake pulls, a knife symbolizes a broken relationship, a severed bond, a future filled with pain and heartache.

This isn't good.

I stare at it, my mind working through the implications. Is this some kind of twisted joke? A cruel prank?

I glance around the circle of smiling faces, trying to gauge their reactions. But they're all too busy cooing over their own charms—a heart for true love, an anchor for stability, a flower for beauty—to notice what's happened.

Except for Monica, who is staring at me expectantly. I force a smile, tucking the knife back into the folds of my napkin. "How lovely," I manage to choke out, my voice brittle. "A knife, how...unique."

She beams at me, oblivious to my discomfort. *Did she have something to do with this?*

"A knife, how perfect. It symbolizes cutting ties with the past and starting something new. Appropriate, especially for a baker, don't you think?"

I'm practically speechless. *Could she be talking about Zach?*

"Where did you get these?" I manage to ask, my voice practically a whisper.

"I had them custom-made by this little shop in Charleston. They're one of a kind, just like our sweet Tucker."

I nod, my throat suddenly dry. *One of a kind, indeed.*

CHAPTER SEVEN

I pull through the gate of Tucker's sprawling estate, the crunch of gravel beneath my tires a welcome sound. After I left the bridal luncheon, I made my way back to the shop to finish the order of baby shower cookies. Bernie had baked each cookie to perfection, then laid them out for me in neat rows, ready for decorating. All I had to do was apply the icing and let them dry overnight.

The whole process only took me a couple of hours, but it drained me of every last bit of energy I had. The thought of Tucker wrapping his tanned arms around me is the only thing keeping me awake at this point.

The landscaped lights flicker on to greet the evening sky, lighting up the house like a castle. As I step out of my car, I take a moment to breathe in the heady scent of magnolia blossoms and freshly cut grass. There's no denying that it's a beautiful property with its grand limestone façade, perfectly manicured bushes, and towering windows. I remind myself how lucky I am to be living here for the past six months—even though it still doesn't quite feel like home.

Tucker moved in here after his grandmother died a couple of years ago, and spent a small fortune redecorating the place. Or I should say, Charlotte redecorated the place, as Monica oh-so-casually mentioned the first time we met. For months, Charlotte worked with an expensive designer, handpicking every detail from the wall colors to the fixtures and fabrics. The end result is breathtaking, straight out of *Southern Living* magazine. But living in a home that's essentially Charlotte's masterpiece leaves a sour taste in my mouth.

Maybe someday I'll hire someone to help me at the shop, so I have time to put my own signature touches on the place. For now, I'm stuck with Charlotte's vision for the property, her presence looming over me like a ghost.

I push the thought aside while I make my way up the front steps, my heels clicking against the polished wood. *This is my home now, for better or worse.*

As I step through the front door, the aroma of bourbon and bitters greets me. Tucker's in the kitchen, his sleeves rolled up and his brow furrowed in concentration as he crafts the perfect cocktail. It's not often that Tucker is waiting for me when I get home. He's usually busy with work, especially the last few months. I often end up alone at the end of the day, having a lonely glass of wine in our cavernous kitchen.

"Welcome home, darlin'," he drawls in his honey-smooth voice. "I figured you could use a little pick-me-up after your big day with the ladies."

I lean across the counter, plucking the glass from his hand and taking a sip. The smooth burn of the bourbon mingles with the sweet tang of citrus. I let out a little moan of appreciation.

"Tucker Harding, you sure do know the way to a woman's heart," I say.

He grins, that lopsided smile that never fails to make my knees go weak. "What can I say? I'm a man of many talents."

I notice a large white gift bag sitting in the center of the island.

"What's this?"

He cocks his head to the side. "Oh nothing, just a little gift for my future wife."

I set my drink down and pull the bag, which is rather heavy, toward me. I tug at the delicate tissue and reach inside to find a crisp white box, with a gold Dior logo emblazoned on the side.

"Tucker, you didn't have to get me anything..."

If there's one thing I can say about my fiancé, it's that he is generous with his gifts. Barely a week passes by when he doesn't gift me with some designer perfume or a new handbag. I can only imagine how many thousands of dollars he's spent on gifts for me. And while I'm not nearly as into the designer goods as most of the women in our social group, I still appreciate the fact that he wants to spoil me.

I pry open the box, revealing a delicate purse adorned with glistening pearl-colored beads that shimmer under the light. "It's beautiful," I say, almost breathless.

"I thought you could wear it to the wedding reception."

I turn the purse in the light. I wasn't lying, it is a beautiful purse. "Thank you," I murmur.

He makes his way around the island, until he's just a few inches in front of me. I set the purse back on the counter as he locks his arms around my waist. I have to push up on my tiptoes to kiss him.

"Only the best for my beautiful bride," he says.

I breathe in the smell of his skin which is mixed with an oaky-scented cologne. Tucker has a way of making me forget about my worries. When his arms are wrapped around me, everything else seems to fade away. We stand there locked in a long kiss for a few minutes, and for a moment I think we might abandon our drinks and head to the bedroom. He pulls away.

"Let's go sit in the living room," he says. "I want to hear all about your day."

The two of us settle onto the large leather sofa. Tucker leans back and I prop my legs up on his lap. I haven't eaten much since the luncheon, and the bourbon is already going to my head.

"So, how did it go today?" he asks, his fingers idly playing with a strand of my hair. "Did Shelby Ann regale you with tales of her latest plastic surgery? Or did Eliza Jane finally admit to sleeping with her tennis instructor?"

I snort, nearly choking on my drink. "You are terrible," I say playfully. "They were...nice."

He raises an eyebrow at me. "Come on, really?"

"Okay, okay... I felt like I was a prized heifer being sized up at the county fair. One wrong move and I'm off to the butcher."

Tucker throws his head back in laughter. "Sounds about right."

"Am I really going to have to socialize with these women for the rest of our lives?"

He reaches over and tucks a strand of hair behind my ear. "They're not so bad, once you get to know them. You just have to realize they're all desperately insecure. And here you are, young and beautiful, with your own bakery. They're probably a little intimidated by you."

"Right, intimidated by me," I say, rolling my eyes dramatically. I can't resist scoffing at the idea that Caroline, with her carefully manicured nails and designer handbag, would be intimidated by *me*. She certainly wasn't intimidated when she brought up Zach.

But I don't want to rain on Tucker's parade. He's so excited about me getting to know his friends. I don't have the heart to tell him that I'd rather have a root canal than spend another minute trying to navigate the minefield of backhanded compliments and thinly veiled insults.

"I was just wondering...has your mother RSVP'd yet?" Tucker asks.

I feel my stomach clench. *My mother. I'd almost forgotten.*

"No, I haven't heard from her," I say, trying to keep my tone casual. "But that doesn't necessarily mean she's not coming. You know how she is—she's not exactly the most reliable when it comes to these things."

"I know," he says, his thumb rubbing soothing circles on my skin. "But I also know how much it would mean to you to have her there."

My mind flashes back to a conversation we had months ago, when we were first starting to plan the wedding. I had been agonizing over whether to even invite my mother, given our strained relationship.

"I just don't know if I can handle the stress of having her there," I had confessed to Tucker. "What if she gets drunk and causes a scene? What if she ruins everything?"

But Tucker had kept pressing me to include her. "Reese, honey, I know it's scary, but I also know that you'll regret it if you don't at least give her the chance to be there for you on your big day."

He had kissed my forehead, his voice soft and reassuring. I had to bite my tongue. It's easy to be optimistic when you haven't experienced the repercussions of an alcoholic mother. I couldn't help but remember her showing up drunk at my school play, or stumbling to the school bus drop-off with smeared makeup, still wearing her clothes from the night before. I thought I'd escaped the embarrassment when I moved down south, but of course, she is still my mother.

"And if she does show up and things get tough," he had continued, "I'll be right there by your side. We'll handle it together."

How could I say no to that? I remember thinking. So, when the gilded invitations went out, I included one for my mother.

Now, sitting here in the living room with the wedding just days away, I wonder if I made the right decision. I know that he's right, that I would probably regret not extending the invitation to my mother.

Probably.

"You're right," I say, squeezing his hand. "I'm glad I invited her, even if she doesn't end up coming. At least I know I did everything I could to include her."

Tucker smiles, his eyes crinkling at the corners. "That's my girl," he says, leaning in to press a soft kiss to my lips. "At the end of the day, all that matters is that we're getting married. The rest is just details." He kisses me again, but this time his kiss feels deeper, hungrier. Just as his hand starts to creep up my thigh, the shrill ring of his phone shatters the moment.

Tucker sighs, pulling away. "Damn it," he says, glancing at the screen. "It's one of my suppliers. I've been trying to track down this shipment for weeks. Just give me a couple of minutes."

I nod, trying to hide my disappointment. Right, work. *Again.*

He makes his way down the hall to his home office. I sigh, getting up from the couch and making my way into the kitchen to make myself a sandwich.

It's not the first time his work has interrupted our alone time. I doubt it'll be the last.

CHAPTER EIGHT

I finish the last few bites of my turkey sandwich and drop my plate into the dishwasher. I can hear Tucker down the hall, his voice low and intense. It doesn't sound like he'll be getting off the call anytime soon.

Tucker's import-export business, Harding Global, is a staggering operation. What started as a small, family-owned business has grown into a multinational corporation with offices in a dozen countries. The heart of the company lies in the port of Charleston, where he oversees a large warehouse complex that hums with activity day and night. Massive shipping containers are loaded and unloaded by a small army of workers that, according to him, need to be babysat day and night. He has a pretty large management team, but it seems like every time I turn around, he's taking a call or running off to handle an emergency.

It's something I truly respect about him, but it also makes our relationship a challenge. With both of us working long hours, it's hard to make quality time for each other.

I decide to head upstairs for a quick shower before bed.

As the hot water cascades down my shoulders, my mind can't help but wander to Charlotte. I find myself wondering what her life with Tucker must have been like, juggling the demands of his thriving empire and the intricacies of their high-society relationship.

I can imagine her spending long hours alone in their sprawling mansion, waiting for Tucker to return from his endless business trips and late-night meetings. Did she feel neglected, pushed aside in favor of his ambitions? Was she constantly competing for his attention, trying to carve out a place for herself in his fast-paced world?

Is that why she left?

I know that Charlotte came from money herself, with a trust fund that would have allowed her to live comfortably without ever lifting a finger. But from what I've heard, she was never content to simply sit back and play the role of the pampered socialite. Instead, she threw herself into charitable work, volunteering her time and resources to various organizations throughout Charleston.

But I also wonder if her philanthropic efforts were somehow tied to her relationship with Tucker. Was it a way for her to distract herself from the loneliness and isolation of being married to a man who was always on the go?

The more I think about it, the more I realize how little I truly know about their relationship. Tucker rarely speaks about Charlotte, and when he does, it's always in vague, dismissive terms. "Things just didn't work out," he'll say with a shrug, as if their entire history can be summed up in a single, throwaway phrase.

But it's more than "things just didn't work out." *She left him at the altar.* For her to do something that cruel to Tucker...something must have caused her to snap.

I shake my head. I shouldn't be thinking about her just a few days before our wedding, but it still bothers me. Not knowing why she left him.

I turn off the water, step out of the shower, and wrap myself in a towel. I busy myself with getting ready for bed, pushing all thoughts of Charlotte to the back of my mind. Dwelling on the past isn't going to help me right now.

I look over at the clock. It's after ten p.m. and Tucker is still on his call. It's moments like these that make me wonder if I'm cut out for this life—the constant interruptions, the never-ending demands on his time and attention. I let out a long sigh as I fall into bed and pull the covers over me.

Just as I begin to drift off to sleep, I hear footsteps on the stairs.

"Listen, we need to handle this now," he hisses, his words barely audible. "If customs gets wind of this, we're all going down. I'm not about to get arrested over some shipping manifest discrepancy."

Arrested? What on earth is he talking about?

There's a pause, and then Tucker's voice again, lower this time, almost a growl. "I don't care how you do it. Just fix it. And make sure there's no paper trail. We can't afford any loose ends."

I chew on my lip. Tucker's business has a lot of moving parts, including the clearance of large shipments from various countries, such as China and Vietnam. He's faced numerous challenges in the past, like when a container of electronics arrived with the wrong customs documentation, causing a week-long delay at the port. I'm sure this is just another one of those situations.

But it's Tucker's tone that unsettles me. The calm,

collected voice I'm used to has vanished, replaced by something I can't quite place.

Before I can add it to the loop of endless anxiety that seems to be plaguing my mind lately, the door creaks open. "Reese," Tucker says, entering the room. "Are you asleep?"

"Almost," I murmur.

I hear Tucker slide out of his clothes. He climbs into bed beside me, his arms wrapping around my waist and pulling me close. "I'm sorry about that. I know I've been distracted lately. It's just work...it's been driving me crazy."

I can still smell the hint of bourbon on his breath and the sweet smell of his skin. Suddenly, all the worries that had been consuming me for the past hour seem unimportant. A little jolt of desire runs through me.

"It's okay. If anyone understands, it's me."

"I don't deserve you," he murmurs, kissing the spot between my neck and my shoulder.

I turn in his arms, pressing a finger to his lips. "Shh, less talking, more showing."

CHAPTER NINE

FOUR DAYS BEFORE THE WEDDING

"No peeking," Bernie scolds as she shoves me out of the kitchen.

"Aw, c'mon, I just want a quick look," I protest, trying to turn my head back into the room even as she keeps pushing me away. "Is everything rising evenly? Did you use enough baking soda?"

"You make it sound like I've never made a wedding cake before." Bernie glares at me. "Now go out front. I already told you, you can see it once we get the first and second layers of buttercream on the cake. Don't you want to be somewhat surprised for your wedding day?"

I roll my eyes. The truth is, *no*, I don't want to be surprised. But if I push her any harder, she'll think I don't trust her. And I do trust Bernie. She's extremely talented and just as capable of producing a perfectly executed wedding cake as I am.

"Fine, I'll go," I say, letting out a sigh. I turn my back on the kitchen and proceed to the front of the shop.

As a bakery owner, it's not often that you have the

chance to make your own wedding cake. Most people would assume I'd go all out with an extravagant creation, perhaps seven layers coated in gold leaf and pearls. But for me, the most romantic cakes are those that pay tribute to the golden era of weddings after World War II. A simple three-tiered white cake adorned with delicate pearls and fresh roses is what truly speaks to me—elegant and simple.

It also doesn't hurt that opting for a simpler design on the cake allows me to focus on *everything else* I have going on this week.

With the museum gala just around the corner, we have set up an extra workstation in our small tasting room near the front of the shop. I stop in the doorway, leaning against the wall to survey the room. There are two long tables set up in the center. Every surface is covered with trays of meticulously crafted petit fours, delicate macarons, and artfully decorated cupcakes. The sweet aroma of vanilla and sugar hangs in the air.

I mentally run through my checklist of everything that must be completed before Saturday. The gold leaf accents on the petit fours need to be finished, the macarons measured so that each matches in size and shape. In keeping with the *Under the Sea* theme, I've created the perfect ombre effect on the cupcakes that transitions from deep blue to a pearly teal. Well, *most* of them are perfect. My shoulders fall as I notice a few that aren't quite right. *I'll have to fix those later.*

Once all the desserts are ready, I'll need to package them securely for transport to the gala venue. I've rented a delivery truck that's bigger than my first apartment, just to ensure that every last macaron and petit four arrives unscathed. And of course, this all has to happen while I'm elbow deep in hairspray and mascara, getting ready for my own trip down the aisle.

Thankfully, Bernie has volunteered to do the delivery with a friend of hers—earlier in the day so she can make it to the wedding in time to see me walk down the aisle.

It's a lot. And it all has to be timed perfectly.

The sound of the front door opening pulls me out of my thoughts. I look up and see a very pregnant woman gliding through the front door. She is impeccably dressed, her blonde hair pulled back in a sleek chignon and her designer handbag gleaming under the soft lights of the bakery.

"Reese Montgomery?"

"Yes," I say, making my way to the front counter. "How can I help you?"

"I'm Cara Dawson. I'm here to pick up an order for a baby shower."

"Of course, Mrs. Dawson, let me get those for you."

"Please, call me Cara. Thank you."

I rush to the back of the bakery and pull a set of pink-and-white-striped boxes from the shelf. Inside are five dozen cookies in diaper and rattle shapes, carefully decorated with white, blue, and silver royal icing.

When I step back up to the counter and place the packages in front of her, I can feel Cara's eyes studying me. Something about her gaze makes my skin prickle.

"It's a bit cold in here," she says, rubbing her upper arms.

"Oh, yes, sorry about that. We have a big event we're preparing for, and sugar melts quickly."

"Hm," she replies.

I point to the boxes. "Would you like to look at the cookies first?"

"Yes, of course," she says. I slide the lid open and reveal the cookies inside.

"Oh, these are perfect!" she says, a smile creasing her eyes. She looks back up at me. "And thank you for putting them together so quickly."

"My pleasure," I say, genuinely pleased that she not only loves the cookies but acknowledges the fact that I had to rush last night to finish them.

I take her credit card and begin to ring up the order. The entire time, I feel her staring at me, like she has something to say. When I hand back her credit card, she clears her throat.

"Don't you have a wedding this Saturday?"

I blush. "I do."

She cocks her head to the side. "Tucker Harding, right?"

I nod. "Do you know him?"

"Yes, I am a friend of Charlotte's."

The words hang in the air between us, heavy with unspoken meaning. The urge to roll my eyes in annoyance is almost overwhelming. *Of course she's friends with Charlotte.* It seems like everyone in this town—heck, probably everyone in the entire city of Charleston—has some connection to Tucker's ex-fiancée.

"Small world," I mutter, not really sure what to say. She reaches forward and begins to gather the boxes, balancing them above her pregnant belly. "Please, let me carry those out for you."

"Oh no, I've got it. Don't worry."

She turns away from me and begins to leave. I maneuver around the front counter and take a few quick strides to pass her before she makes it to the front door. I reach the door just as she approaches, my hand grasping the handle and pulling it open. She steps forward to pass me, her heels clicking on the polished wood floor, but something makes her pause.

When she turns to face me, her green eyes glint with a mixture of emotions I can't quite decipher.

"You know, Charlotte called me in a panic two nights before her wedding to Tucker," she says. "She told me she had something important to tell me about him, but she wanted to wait until she was sure."

"Oh?" I manage to choke out, my heart hammering in my chest. *Why is she telling me this?*

She nods, her eyes narrowing. "She seemed upset, almost frightened. But before she could tell me more, she got another phone call and had to rush off."

A tremor ripples through me as I process yet another unsettling piece of information about Tucker's former fiancée. My mind races with a thousand questions. *What was so important? Why did she have to make sure? Why was she upset?*

I try to collect myself and keep calm, burying the questions that are running through my mind. Discussing Tucker's ex with a customer is beyond inappropriate, even if she is the one who brought it up. I force a strained smile at Cara.

"Well, I'm sure whatever it was, it's in the past now."

Cara shrugs her shoulders. "That's actually the last time I spoke to her. Don't you think that's strange?"

You have no idea.

"A little," I say, my voice coming out in a squeak.

She hesitates for a moment longer, her gaze locked with mine as an uncomfortable silence fills the room. In that brief moment, it's like I can see the secrets swirling behind her eyes. I want to reach out, to grab her by the shoulders and demand that she tell me everything she knows about Charlotte's disappearance.

But I don't. Because as much as I'm desperate for answers, I barely know this woman. And let's be honest, the only person I should be talking to about Charlotte is *Tucker*. I think back to all the times I've tried to broach the subject, only to be met with stony silence or evasive non-answers. It's the one topic that's always been off-limits, the one part of his past that he guards with a fierce intensity.

But why? What could have happened between them that was so terrible he can't bear to speak of it?

Finally, she looks away and shakes her head once more.

"You know, I probably shouldn't have brought it up. I'm sure you have plenty on your mind before the big day." She turns back to the doorway and steps outside. "It was nice to meet you, Reese!" she calls over her shoulder.

"You too," I say quietly as she ambles down the sidewalk. I stare after her for a moment longer, standing frozen in the doorway, the questions lingering in my mind.

CHAPTER TEN

"What was that all about?" Bernie asks as she enters the room, her eyebrows raised in a mixture of curiosity and concern.

I bite my lip for a second longer, stewing over the encounter.

The truth is, *I'd love to tell her.*

I'd love to sit Bernie down and explain how the ghost of Charlotte has been following me and Tucker around since our first date. How I can't seem to escape this woman from his past. How every customer who walks into my shop either knew her personally or they've heard about how she left Tucker at the altar. How I had to toss out a dozen monogramed pillows scattered throughout the house with her name on them. Or how every restaurant in town gives us Tucker's "special" table—he's never said anything but I know that's where he and Charlotte used to sit. And the funny look the waitress gives me when she shows up to the table confirms it—she clearly was expecting someone else.

It's like everywhere I turn, there's another reminder of

the woman who came before me, the one who seemingly had it all—the perfect relationship, the stunning home, the charmed life. And then she up and disappeared, the day of her fairy-tale wedding.

How it's all very *weird*. Just thinking about it makes my palms sweat.

But even as the urge to confide in Bernie grows stronger, I force myself to swallow it back. Our relationship has always been light and easy, a refuge from the complicated social web that seems to ensnare everyone else in this town. She's the one person I can talk to without feeling the heaviness of Charlotte's memory bearing down on me, the one friend who sees me for who I am rather than whom I'm trying to replace.

And I'm not ready to let go of that, not yet.

"Oh, nothing," I say instead, smoothing down the front of my apron with hands that tremble slightly. "That was just Cara Dawson, the woman who ordered the baby shower cookies yesterday."

Bernie's face lights up. "Oh, great! So, what did she think? Did she love them?"

I force a smile onto my face, hoping it looks more convincing than it feels. "She did, actually. You did a fabulous job, Bernie. Thanks again."

The words feel hollow, a flimsy cover for my internal struggle. But Bernie just beams, her cheeks flushing with pleasure.

"It's nothing," she says, waving a hand dismissively. Then she turns her face toward the tasting room. "So, how's it going with the gala prep?"

"Come on, I'll show you."

We walk over to the tasting room where I have the makeshift workroom set up for the big gala. I walk her through each pastry, and my thoughts behind the design. She nods and listens, interjecting a few suggestions here and there. When I'm finally done, she pats me on the shoulder.

"Everything looks fabulous," she says. "You've outdone yourself, Reese."

Now it's my turn to beam with pride. Her face suddenly falls. "But don't we need to get these into the freezer?"

My shoulders fall. As I told Cara, we've had to crank the air conditioning in the shop while we wait for the repairman to come and fix the walk-in cooler. Meanwhile, I've loaded everything I could into the freezer, hoping it thaws out properly and doesn't lose its shape or color before the gala on Saturday.

"You're right. I'm still waiting on the repairman. For now, these go into the freezer."

Bernie just nods, her expression sympathetic. "Hey, whatever works. You're doing great, Reese. Now, I should get back to the wedding cake I've been working on. The customer is a real bridezilla."

She gives me a good-natured nudge. I smile. "Thanks. Let me know if you need anything."

Bernie turns and heads back into the bakery area. I busy myself with the final details of the macarons, forcing myself to focus on my work and not think about what Cara Dawson said.

About thirty minutes later, the front bell rings again. I tuck a few pieces of hair behind my ears and grab a towel to wipe my hands before heading out front.

When I see who's waiting there, I let out a sigh of relief. Standing in the front of the shop is a round man with a uniform that reads "Freddy's Freezer Repair."

"Oh, you must be here to repair the walk-in cooler. Your

timing is perfect!" I quickly march across the room to enthu-
siastically shake his hand. "I'm Reese Montgomery."

"Charlie," he says, shaking my hand with his own pudgy
ones. "Where's the cooler you need fixed?"

I'm slightly taken back by his frankness, but regardless, I
lead him to the back of the bakery where we have a large
walk-in cooler unit.

"It's been giving us trouble since last month, but it
completely quit a few days ago."

"Got it," he says. "I'll get started right away."

I fumble with the waistband of my apron. "The thing is,
I really need to have it fixed today. We have a big gala
coming up, and I'm blasting the air conditioning just to keep
the pastries chilled. I'd love to be able to get these inside the
cooler before I have to leave at the end of the day."

He stares at me, no emotion or expression on his face.

"I'll do my best."

My heart drops. I was hoping for more confidence on his
part. The real truth is I need the cooler fixed *yesterday*. The
freezer is running out of room and I can only imagine what
my electric bill next month is going to be with all the air
conditioning I've been blasting through the shop.

"Thank you so much. I mean it," I say.

I leave him to work and head back up into my office to
check on some invoices. I pull out my phone and notice I
have a couple of message notifications. Before I get to the
invoices, I swipe them open.

The first message comes from an app called Snaptalk,
which I haven't used in months. Bernie installed it on my
phone last summer, insisting we could use it to send each
other funny messages that vanish after sixty seconds. I tap on
the notification, which says I have a message from Snap-

per2344. When the message loads, my breath catches in my throat, and a chill runs down my spine.

It reads:

Don't marry Tucker. He is a murderer. You have four days to call off the wedding.

CHAPTER ELEVEN

I stand frozen in the middle of my office, staring at my phone while the air conditioning hums loudly in the background. I wait a beat too long and the screen suddenly goes dark. I swipe it open again and quickly navigate to my messages. When I do, the message that was there just a moment ago is gone. I try to click through the profile, looking for Snapper... but I can't remember the numbers and nothing under that name comes up.

What in the world? Did I just imagine that?

I shake my head. No, I didn't imagine it. Someone sent me a message saying Tucker is a murderer, of all things. Who would send a message like that? More importantly, *why?*

I raise my eyes to the front door where Cara Dawson left about thirty minutes ago. Could she have sent this message? I have her phone number on the invoice. Maybe I should call her. I shuffle through a stack of papers and pull out the invoice for the baby shower cookie order. I run my fingers over the page until I pinpoint her phone number.

I start punching her number into my phone. And then I

stop, my thumb suspended over the call button. *What am I doing?* If I call Cara Dawson and ask her if she sent me a message saying Tucker's a murderer, she's going to think I've lost my mind. And I'm sure she'll be happy to share that little piece of gossip with everyone around town.

I rub my temples. *No, I need to figure this out on my own.* Maybe this whole wedding is getting to me and I'm losing my mind.

I think back to everything I know about Charlotte's disappearance, every hushed whisper that has followed me since the day Tucker and I got together. *Where did Charlotte go? I heard she ran away with a boat captain. Did you know she was taking French lessons? I bet she flew off to the south of France. Well, I heard she had a mental breakdown and had to be put in an institution.* Then they'd turn to Tucker. *Poor Tucker. I heard he lost a small fortune on that wedding.*

People don't think I can hear them whispering about me, but I can. And it's infuriating. After the whispers stop, they usually give me a side-eye, like somehow I'm "in the know" on the whole situation. Which I am obviously *not*.

I suppose Mrs. Spencer must know what happened, as I'm sure she's been in touch with her daughter. I wish she would just set the record straight and cut through all the mystery surrounding what happened that day. That would make my life so much easier.

But if she hasn't come forward by now and told the truth, I doubt she ever will.

I shake my head. I've tried so hard to push it all aside, to focus on the future and the love that Tucker and I share. But clearly I'm not doing myself any favors. Every time I try to bury what happened between the two of them, fate seems to step in and send me a sign. Or in this case, a text message.

I mean, who sends a message like that?

Tucker is not a murderer. The very idea is ludicrous, like something out of a poorly plotted movie. The man who rubs my feet after a long day or sends me flowers "just because" is not someone who would murder his fiancée. People here *know* Tucker. He's part of the community, a member of every local society. And someone whom everyone knows as an upstanding citizen doesn't even attempt to commit murder, much less get away with it.

I lean heavily against my desk, my legs suddenly weak beneath me. I wish everyone would just stop bringing up Charlotte, stop dredging up the painful memories and unanswered questions that have haunted me for so long.

I stare at my phone for a few seconds longer.

What am I going to do?

As if on cue, another message appears on Snaptalk. This time it's from Zach.

How are you holding up? Do you need anything?

He has no idea. Or maybe he does.

Zach was always pretty intuitive. He always seemed to know what was going on in my head. I bite my lip, torn between the desire to confide in someone and the fear of betraying Tucker's trust. But as I stare at Zach's message, I can't shake the feeling that he might be the only person who can truly understand what I'm going through. Maybe it wouldn't hurt to call him.

Just as I pull my fingers into place to send him a message in return, I hear the door open at the front of the shop. Maybe Cara Dawson has come back to get a copy of her receipt and I can casually ask her more questions about

Charlotte. I slide my phone back into my pocket and head toward the front. When I arrive behind the counter, I'm surprised to see Tucker himself striding into the shop, a boyish grin on his face.

"There's my beautiful bride-to-be!" he exclaims, swooping around the counter and pulling me in for a kiss. "Everything okay?" He pulls back with a concerned expression on his face.

"Yes, of course. Just busy."

He runs his hands through my hair. "I thought I'd surprise you with lunch. Can you get away for an hour?"

I reflexively glance back at the table behind me filled with rows of pastries. And then back at him. Truthfully? No. But I have a hard time refusing my handsome fiancé anything. Besides, maybe it's time I talk to him about everything that's been going on.

"Sure," I say.

"Wonderful," he says, a smile spreading across his face. "By the way, I just ran into Cara Dawson shopping down the street. She told me she just picked up a few dozen beautiful cookies from your shop for her baby shower."

"Yes, she was very sweet," I say. Even though I know the answer to my next question, I can't resist testing Tucker a bit. "How did you know her?"

"Oh, you know, just friends of friends," he says. A flicker of something crosses his eyes and then passes.

I stare at him for a moment, raising my eyebrows. *Friends of friends?* I know exactly how he knows Cara Dawson. I reflexively take a step back. It's not a lie, per se, but an omission of the truth. She was a friend of *Charlotte's*. Why wouldn't he admit that? A little seed of doubt is planted in my mind.

I know that bringing up Charlotte will only make him angry. The last thing I need to do is get in a fight with my fiancé just a few days before our wedding, especially over his ex.

But I can't help myself.

"Actually, she told me she was a friend of Charlotte's," I say carefully, watching Tucker's reaction like a hawk, "and that Charlotte was a bridesmaid in her wedding."

Tucker's face hardens, his eyes narrowing as he pulls away from me.

"Charlotte?" he repeats, his voice tight. "Why would you bring her up, Reese? You know how much it hurts me to talk about her."

A tiny stab of guilt gnaws at me, mixed with a growing sense of unease. I'm sure it was painful, standing at the altar in front of hundreds of friends and family, wondering where she was. I can't even imagine the humiliation he must have felt, the way his heart must have dropped into his stomach as the minutes ticked by and the realization slowly dawned on him that she wasn't coming. He must have felt like a fool, standing there in his perfectly tailored tuxedo, a hopeful smile plastered on his face even as the whispers and murmurs began to ripple through the crowd. I can picture him ducking out of the church, his head bowed and his shoulders slumped, trying to avoid the pitying stares and the well-meaning condolences.

It's no wonder he doesn't want to talk about it. The wounds of that day must still be raw, even after all this time. And part of me can't blame him for wanting to keep that pain locked away, for not wanting to relive the most devastating moment of his life.

At the same time, I can't shake the feeling that there's

more to the story than he's letting on. Especially when I get messages like the one I received today, or at least I *think* I received today...

"I'm sorry," I mumble, looking down at my flour-dusted hands. "I just thought it was strange, that's all. That she felt the need to let me know she was a friend of Charlotte's."

Tucker sighs heavily, his face softening. He cups my shoulders in his hands.

"Look, Reese, I know you're stressed about the wedding and the gala. But please, can we just focus on us? On our future together? I don't want to dwell on the past anymore."

I nod slowly, trying to ignore the sinking feeling in my gut. "You're right," I say, forcing a brittle smile. "I'm sorry I brought it up. Let's just enjoy our lunch."

"Thank you." He pulls me in for a hug. I briefly melt into his arms, letting myself feel the warmth of his body and the musky scent of his cologne. I stay there for almost a full minute.

"Let me grab my purse in the back," I say, finally slipping away from him.

As I walk back to the office to snag my purse, I pull out my phone. I stare at the screen for a split second, looking at Zach's message.

The truth is, I'm not okay. Tucker has shut me down again, leaving me with no one I can talk to. Except Zach. So against my better judgment, I shoot him a message.

Actually it's been a rough day. Would you be free to grab coffee at Marla's this afternoon?

The answer is swift.

Of course. 3pm?

I give his message the thumbs-up before squeezing my phone back into my purse. I swipe on some lip gloss before heading back out to the bakery where Tucker is waiting. But as I let him lead me out of the bakery, his hand warm and solid in mine, I can't shake the nagging sense that everything is about to come crashing down around me.

CHAPTER TWELVE

It's me who spots her first.

Tucker and I are casually walking down Main Street on the way to lunch when I see her approaching. At first I don't recognize her, her face half-covered by a pair of large black sunglasses. It's the crisp tweed suit that gives her away, even though it's hanging off her thin frame like it belongs to someone else. She pulls down her glasses to peek into a window display, and when I see the unmistakable blue eyes, I know it's her.

Amanda Spencer, *Charlotte's mother*.

Tucker's grip tightens around my hand. I know he sees her too.

She looks different, to say the least. Her face is gaunt, the space under her eyes dark. And she's disturbingly thin. I can practically count the bones on her hand as she grips her designer bag. Just as she is about to pass us, I hesitate. And before I can stop myself, I call out, "Mrs. Spencer?"

She stops, turning to face us with a start. For a moment, confusion flickers across her face, and then recognition dawns. "Miss Montgomery," she says, her voice a raspy whisper. "And...Tucker."

Tucker stiffens beside me, pulling me closer. He nods curtly, his eyes fixed on a point just over Amanda's shoulder. "Mrs. Spencer," he mutters, barely audible.

It's been over a year since I've seen her, not since the fateful day we met at my shop to discuss the wedding cake. The memory of the day slams into me, making all the ghosts that have been following me around the last few months suddenly more real. Clearly Charlotte leaving town has broken the woman in front of me. Her eyes look empty and her figure gaunt.

An uncomfortable silence descends, thick and heavy. What is likely a few seconds of silence crawls past like an hour. I open my mouth at least twice before speaking, all the unanswered questions at the tip of my tongue... *What happened to Charlotte? Why did she leave Tucker at the altar? Where is she now?*

I scramble to find something else to say, as this clearly isn't the time or place to launch into a conversation about the past. Especially given the jilted groom is currently holding my hand.

"How...how have you been?" I ask, immediately regretting the banality of the question.

Amanda's lips curve into a smile that doesn't reach her eyes. "Oh, you know," she says, waving a bony hand dismissively. "Keeping busy. And you two? I hear congratulations are in order."

The way her eyes narrow when she says those last words makes my stomach knot up. Heat rises up my cheeks. "Yes, thank you."

Tucker is deathly silent next to me. I can barely hear him

breathing. I look at him out of the corner of my eyes, willing him to say something, anything, to break the awkward silence, but he continues to stand perfectly still. Amanda seems to be waiting for him to say something as well, so the three of us just end up standing there in unbearable silence.

Finally, Amanda clears her throat. "Well, I won't keep you," she says, already turning away. "Congratulations, again."

And just like that, she's gone, disappearing into the crowd of tourists and locals that throng the sidewalk. I immediately turn to Tucker, my heart racing. He's still gripping my hand, but his eyes are fixed in the distance, where Amanda just left. I search his face for any clue to his thoughts, but his face is blank.

"Tucker? Are you alright?"

He furrows his brow and then turns to face me. He blinks twice, as if his eyes are adjusting to the light, and then shrugs. "I'm fine. Come on, let's go to lunch," he says, tugging gently on my hand.

We walk in silence for another half-block before we reach the restaurant. By the time we make it inside, Tucker is back to himself, making small talk with the hostess.

I, on the other hand, am a ball of nerves. I can't shake the image of Amanda's haunted eyes or her frail figure. She was not the confident, domineering woman whom I met a year ago in my shop.

What happened to her?

We settle into our seats, and the waiter greets our table, leaving us with a menu. Once the water glasses have been filled, I tip my menu down and look at Tucker.

"Is that the first time you've seen her since...?"

He looks back at me, tipping his head to the side. "Who?"

"Amanda Spencer," I say, a bit of irritation creeping into my voice.

He glares back down at his menu. "Drop it, Reese."

I twist my menu in my hands, my cheeks burning. He's shutting me out, *again*. And what about the message I received earlier? I was hoping to share that with him. But now?

I open my mouth to speak, but the waiter shows up as if on cue to take our order. After she leaves, Tucker immediately turns the conversation to the wedding, leaving me no room to talk about everything else that's been happening. I fiddle with the napkin in my lap. How can he be so dismissive? Don't I deserve answers about what happened?

I listen to him chatter on about the wedding, my mind completely somewhere else. If the encounter with Amanda bothered him, he's very good at hiding it.

Eventually I soften, allowing myself to get swept up in his enthusiasm. His excitement for the wedding is genuine. I tell myself that nothing good is going to come from dwelling on the past. I let go of my indignation over his dismissal of the topic. *For now*. Maybe I'll bring up the cryptic text message to him later tonight.

When the check comes, I feel a sense of relief. I need a moment to myself to try and piece everything together in my head. As he kisses me on the sidewalk and we go our separate ways, a sense of dread coils in my stomach. A gulf is widening between us—I can feel it.

I just hope it's pre-wedding jitters and not something else.

CHAPTER THIRTEEN

A few hours later, I walk into Marla's. I scan the room, which is surprisingly busy for this time of the day. Apparently everyone is in need of a caffeine pick-me-up to ward off the afternoon slump. I spot Zach sitting at a corner table, his soft brown hair falling into his eyes as he scrolls through his phone. He looks up as I approach, a smile spreading across his face.

"Well, well, if it isn't the blushing bride herself," he quips, his eyes twinkling. "To what do I owe the pleasure of this clandestine meeting?"

"Very funny." I roll my eyes, sliding into the seat across from him. He's already ordered me a latte, which is perfectly frothed. I take a grateful sip.

"Thank you for the coffee."

"Of course."

I settle back into my chair and cast my eyes around the room, searching for a familiar face. Thankfully, I don't recognize anyone I know. Zach watches me patiently. I turn back to meet his gaze. "You know this isn't easy for me. I feel like I'm going behind Tucker's back just by being here."

"I'm just here as your friend. And I will be happy to tell Tucker that if needed. But if you really feel that way, then whatever is bothering you must be important."

I let out a long sigh. "There have been some strange things happening lately."

"Strange how?"

"Well, for one, we just ran into Amanda Spencer."

He scrunches his brows together and curls his lip. "Eh, I bet that was awkward."

"You have no idea."

"What did you say? What did Tucker say?"

"Nothing really," I say, skipping the part where Tucker shut me down when I brought it up at lunch. "She congratulated us and went on her way."

He shrugs. "Well, at least you got that out of the way."

"Yeah, I guess."

Zach's right, I should be relieved. In some ways, her words of congratulations should bring me a sense of closure. It *should,* but closure is the last thing I feel.

"I also got a visit today from Cara Dawson."

He immediately rolls his eyes. "Oh yes, I know Cara. Loves gossip as much as her designer shoe collection. She's a piece of work."

"Yes, well, she came in to get some baby shower cookies today and brought up the night before Charlotte and Tucker's wedding."

"Really?"

"Really. She said Charlotte called her two nights before the wedding and told her she had something to tell her about Tucker. But Charlotte wanted to confirm all the details before she shared it with her. Cara mentioned Charlotte sounded scared, then abruptly hung up." I look down at my coffee mug. "That was the last time Cara heard from Charlotte."

The creases in Zach's forehead deepen. "Now that is strange."

I continue, "Then about thirty minutes later I get the weirdest message on Snaptalk. It's from an unknown number and it says, and I quote, 'Don't marry Tucker. He is a murderer. You have four days to call off the wedding.'"

Zach gets a strange look on his face, then shakes his head. "Tucker a murderer? I don't see it."

"Obviously not," I say. "Or I wouldn't be marrying him. But it all just feels really strange. And did they really think I would call off the wedding?"

"Did you check the Snaptalk profile? To see who it was?"

"I tried, but I couldn't remember the username. So..." I pull back, throw up my hands in defeat, and sink down into my chair. Zach reaches forward to comfort me by touching my arm. I let out a tiny sigh.

"Well, someone is messing with you for sure. Someone who doesn't want to see you marrying Tucker," he says.

I take another sip of my coffee, gently pulling my arm away. If anyone saw us here, Zach and I together, his arm on mine, it wouldn't look good.

I've been floating around a list of people who might not want to see me married. But only one name keeps popping up. I take a deep breath, steadying myself before I ask the next question.

"Do you think Charlotte is back?" I whisper, my voice trembling. I think about bumping into her mother today, the forlorn look in her eyes, like she was lost. "Do you think she sent me that message?"

Zach leans back in his chair, his brow furrowed in thought. "It's possible," he says slowly, his fingers drumming a steady rhythm on the tabletop. "Charlotte left Tucker at the altar, yes, but have we ever considered why?"

Only about every other day.

"I've wondered..."

He leans in. "What if she ran because she discovered something...something dangerous?"

"Like what?"

"I don't know." He shrugs. "But it could explain why she's reaching out now, and in such a roundabout way. If she thought Tucker was...involved in something criminal, even dangerous..."

"Like murder?"

He nods grimly. "If that's true, she might be trying to warn you without putting herself at risk. It would explain everything—why she ran, why she's been silent since last year, and why she's choosing this moment to reach out."

I shake my head, feeling like we're grasping at straws. The idea that Charlotte ran away because she discovered Tucker was involved in someone's murder seems pretty unrealistic. On the other hand, Charlotte running away because she fell in love with someone else seems much more plausible.

"I don't know, it seems pretty far-fetched."

The two of us sit in silence for a few minutes, sipping our coffees while the sounds of the café hum around us. I look around the room, as if something might spark an idea. A mother multitasks, feeding her child a muffin with one hand while balancing a book in the other. Nearby, a man frowns at his laptop screen, deep in concentration. At a corner table, a young couple exchanges shy glances, the awkward energy of a first date palpable even from a distance.

They all seem so *normal*.

For a moment, I long for that normalcy, for problems no more serious than a fussy child or a difficult work project. Unfortunately, my problems are much bigger. With a sigh, I return my focus to Zach.

"So, what should I do about the message?"

"Ignore it, for now," he says. "Whoever sent it is just trying to mess with you. You know Tucker better than anyone, so trust your gut. The person who sent that just wants to see you freak out. Charlotte is ancient history. Don't let it get to you."

I blow some air from my lips and sink into my chair. "Easier said than done. Every time I walk in the front door of the house, I feel like she's staring back at me."

He smirks. "I've heard she was quite the decorator."

I roll my eyes.

"What does Tucker think—have you talked to him about all of this? About Charlotte?"

I sigh, fumbling with the handle of my coffee cup. "I've tried. But he always shuts me down. He says it's too painful to talk about."

Zach leans forward, his eyes intense. "Do you trust Tucker?"

I blink, taken aback by the question. "Yes, of course," I say automatically, my heart clenching at the thought.

"Okay, then you two should be able to talk about this. If he knows how much it's bothering you, surely he'll come around. I mean, you can't start a marriage without being able to communicate."

"I know... I just don't want to bother him."

"He's your fiancé, Reese. It's his job to be bothered."

"I know. It's just..." *Easier said than done.*

He looks at me, his expression turning serious. "Are you having cold feet? Because..."

"No," I say, shaking my head. "I'm sure he's the one."

Zach raises his eyebrows and lets his shoulders fall. "Okay, then try to focus on what's important. Your wedding, your future together. Don't let the ghosts of the past ruin what you have now."

I take a deep breath, feeling the knot in my stomach slowly unraveling. "You're right," I say, a small smile tugging at my lips. "I've been so caught up in all this drama that I've forgotten to focus on what really matters."

I reach over to touch Zach's hand, and he reaches his across the table and gives mine a squeeze. For a quick moment, I miss the simplicity of dating him. There was no drama, no runaway bride, and no wedding to plan. I catch myself lingering on that thought a bit too long and pull back my hand.

"Thank you."

Zach laughs, his eyes crinkling at the corners. "Hey, what are friends for?"

We chat for a little while longer, the conversation turning to lighter topics like the gala preparations and the latest gossip from the Charleston social scene. By the time we finish our coffee, a weight has been lifted from my shoulders.

Zach stands to leave, saying he needs to head back to his office. He leans down to give me a quick peck on the cheek. I turn my head slightly and he ends up kissing me partly on the mouth. The brief contact sends a small, familiar flutter through my stomach. I let out an awkward laugh, and he smiles at me before turning toward the door.

It's a small moment, but it leaves me feeling a bit guilty. It's exactly the type of thing Tucker would be furious about.

I give myself a few minutes to savor the last sips of my coffee, trying to hold on to the fleeting sense of calm that our conversation has brought me. When I eventually let my gaze wander around the room, the momentary peace I found with Zach suddenly evaporates.

Sitting in the corner of the café is none other than the queen bee herself.

Monica Harding.

She's deep in conversation with a woman whose back is turned to me, but I can feel her gaze on me like a physical force. When she sees me looking, she raises a perfectly arched eyebrow and nods in my direction. I give her an awkward wave, my heart hammering in my chest. I quickly gather my purse and head toward the door.

As I step out into the bright sunlight, I can feel the panic rising in my throat. Monica doesn't miss a thing. And if she just watched me having a cozy coffee date with my ex-boyfriend, not to mention the accidental kiss, mere days before my wedding to her cousin?

Well, let's just say that the fallout with Tucker would be catastrophic.

CHAPTER FOURTEEN

THREE DAYS BEFORE THE WEDDING

The next day, I throw myself into my work at the shop, channeling all of my energy into finalizing the gala order. Apparently Charlie is a man of action rather than words, because he did manage to fix the walk-in cooler, allowing me to carefully load all the finished pastries inside for Saturday's delivery.

With Bernie taking the lead on my wedding cake, I find myself with a rare bit of breathing room. In fact, the only thing left to do is the invoicing, a task that I usually dread but now feels like a welcome distraction. I spend most of the day doing just that and, of course, trying to avoid thinking about the wedding, Charlotte, Zach, and Monica.

It works, *for the most part.*

Tucker has his bachelor party tonight with the boys at a bourbon distillery in downtown Charleston, leaving me to my own devices. Which is really the last thing I want right now. I don't want to be alone and have more time to stew over everything that's going on.

I need to stay busy.

So, instead of sitting at home by myself, I invite Bernie over to drink champagne, eat tapas, and binge-watch the newest season of *Chopped*. It should be enough to keep my mind off things.

I retrieve a bottle of champagne from the wine chiller and uncork it with a satisfying pop. I carefully pour two glasses. As I watch the bubbles float up to the top of my champagne glass, I'm torn. This should be a celebration—I'm about to pull off the biggest weekend of events Couture Cakes has ever had. Yet, a gnawing sense of dread tugs at me.

Before I can spiral into another loop of negative thoughts, the doorbell rings. I take a deep breath, pick up the champagne glasses, and stride toward the front entry, forcing a smile.

"Bernie, I'm so happy you made it," I say, swinging open the door and handing her a glass.

"Now that's the way to kick off the night." She grins. Bernie's wearing a black lounge set and sneakers, her hair down in loose, pretty waves. I can't remember the last time I saw her hair like that. Usually, we've both got our hair pulled back in a hairnet, making sure no stray hairs end up in someone's dessert.

It's nice to see her let her hair down, literally and figuratively. We spend so much time being super professional, it's easy to forget we're friends too, not just co-workers. And right now, a friend is exactly what I need. I feel a few knots in my shoulders ease.

The two of us walk into the kitchen, champagne flutes in hand. We fill our plates with an assortment of tapas I ordered from a local restaurant. I breathe in the delicious smells and for a moment, I forget about all the thoughts that have been following me around like a dark cloud.

Once our plates are full, we settle in the living room where I grab the remote to flip on the TV. I've cued up our favorite cooking challenge show, *Chopped*. As the first episode begins, Bernie and I start poking fun at the contestants.

"Oh, look at that chef's face when he opened his basket!" Bernie exclaims, pointing at the screen. "It's like he just found out his secret ingredient is roadkill!"

I burst out laughing, nearly spilling my champagne. "Honestly, I don't know how they come up with this stuff. If someone handed me a basket full of gummy worms and fish sauce, I think I'd just walk right out the door."

"Not me," Bernie says, a mischievous glint in her eye. "I'd whip up a gummy worm ceviche with a fish sauce foam, just to see the look on the judges' faces."

"You'd win that round for sure," I say.

By the time the first episode ends, my face hurts from laughing so much. The two of us agree it's time for a refill of champagne. We hop up from the couch and amble into the kitchen.

"Your kitchen is fabulous," Bernie says, looking around the room.

"Thank you," I say quietly, my voice barely above a whisper.

But even as the words leave my lips, I feel a twinge of discomfort. It is beautiful, but all I see in the brass cabinet knobs and intricately patterned backsplash is the woman who lived here first.

"So, are you feeling excited about the wedding?"

"Yes," I say, forcing a smile onto my face. "And nervous."

"You have nothing to be nervous about. I'm sure Elsa has everything planned down to the second."

"Oh, she does," I say, rolling my eyes with a wry smile.

Elsa Patterson, the wedding planner extraordinaire, flew in from New York to orchestrate our big day. At first, I was a bit hesitant about the idea of having someone else plan my wedding. I mean, isn't that supposed to be the bride's job? But when I realized how big of a deal having a large, extravagant wedding was to Tucker, I was glad that Elsa had stepped in to take over.

"Speaking of the wedding, I think I'll have the wedding cake ready for you to look at tomorrow."

"Really?"

"Yup," she says with a wink. "Luckily for us, I didn't have to use any gummy worms or roadkill. It's all flour, sugar, and butter."

"What a relief," I chuckle, feeling a little buzz from my wine. "I can't wait to see it."

Despite all the heaviness that has been surrounding me the last couple of days, I do feel a bit of a flutter of excitement about the cake. Even though I've done hundreds of wedding cakes, there is still a little part of me that can't wait for my little girl dreams to become reality. I refill both of our glasses with champagne, emptying out the bottle.

"Why don't you go in and get the next episode started," I say, walking toward the wine cooler in the butler's pantry. "I'm going to put another bottle on ice for us."

"Sounds perfect," says Bernie.

I pull out a bottle of champagne and drop it in a bucket of ice. No sooner has Bernie disappeared than my phone starts to buzz on the table. Holding my glass, I pick it up and make my way toward the living room. It's most likely a text from Tucker, updating me on his eventful night. But when I unlock my phone, I realize it's a message from Snaptalk.

My heart begins to beat a bit faster. I stop in the hallway and read the message, this time from a new profile called Snapper2345.

Has Tucker told you about his little side business yet? You're not marrying who you think you are. Only three days left to call off the wedding, or else.

The cold plastic of the phone slips slightly in my grasp. I set down my glass on a table in the hall and quickly type a message back.

Who is this?

As soon as I hit send, the message vanishes, leaving me to stare at a blank screen. I desperately search for the username Snapper2345 but nothing comes up.

How could they delete their profile so quickly?

I take a deep, shuddering breath, trying to calm myself. The phone feels suddenly heavy in my hand, like a lead weight. I continue staring at it for a few more minutes, half expecting it to light up again with another message. But the screen stays dark.

What side business? And who in the world is sending these messages? I'm so frustrated I feel like I could punch a hole in the wall.

Bernie's going to wonder what's taking me so long. I slip my phone back into my pocket. I can't let her see me like this. As much as I'd like to spend the next hour combing through Snaptalk for a clue, I know I can't leave her waiting. I take another deep breath, squaring my shoulders and forcing a smile onto my face. It feels brittle and false, like a mask that doesn't quite fit, but it's the best I can do in the moment.

I walk back into the living room, the plush carpet cushioning my footsteps. Bernie looks up, her face quickly changing from a smile to concern.

"Everything okay, Reese? You look a little pale."

"Oh yeah, I'm fine." I force a smile and steady my voice. "I just got a message from Tucker. I think he might be a little bit drunk already."

Bernie smiles. "Boys will be boys."

I settle in next to Bernie on the couch, trying to focus on the TV screen in front of us. But even as the familiar theme music of *Chopped* fills the room, my mind is elsewhere, spinning with a thousand unanswered questions.

Why would someone be sending these messages?

I can't wrap my head around it, can't make sense of the twisted logic that would drive someone to do something like this. Zach's words about Charlotte from earlier echo in my mind. If she wanted to warn me about something, she could just come and tell me about it in person. He's right, of course —there's no reason to send some cryptic messages, other than just to drive me mad.

So if it's not her, then who?

Someone doesn't want me to marry Tucker, obviously. Or at the very least, they want to make my life a living hell. But who would do something like that?

Is it someone from his past, some scorned lover or bitter enemy who can't bear to see him happy with someone else? Or is it someone closer to home, someone who knows me, who has seen the cracks and fissures in our relationship and is determined to exploit them?

It's like I'm going crazy, like I'm trapped in some kind of

waking nightmare where nothing makes sense and everyone is a suspect. I can feel the paranoia creeping in, the sense that I shouldn't trust anyone.

As I glance over at Bernie, sitting next to me, happily lost in watching the show, I realize I'm probably letting my imagination run a little wild. The three glasses of champagne I've had don't help either. I try to push the doubts aside, but I can't shake the feeling that there's something I'm missing.

We finish a few more episodes and get about one glass each into the next bottle when Bernie announces she's tired and doesn't want to be out too late since she has an early day tomorrow. I'm relieved, since I've been holding it together for the last hour trying not to freak out about the latest message.

I walk her to the door, close it behind her, and put my back up against the other side. What am I going to do about these messages? I have to do *something*.

I clean the kitchen, finishing off the last of the bottle of wine, and then sit at the large marble island to stew over my situation. This doesn't help. I try to distract myself by scrolling through Pinterest wedding cakes (one of my favorite pastimes), but that doesn't do the trick either. About an hour later, I hear the door open.

Tucker's home, and it's time we have a talk.

CHAPTER FIFTEEN

As soon as Tucker enters the kitchen, I already know this is horrible timing for what I'm about to say. His shirt is unbuttoned and his tie loosened around his neck. I can see his eyes are slightly glassy. And I can smell the bourbon on his breath even before he reaches me from around the kitchen island.

"Reese, you're awake," he says, his words slightly slurred. "I'm so glad I got to get to see you."

He immediately closes the distance between us, sliding his arms around my waist and pulling me in for a kiss. I let him kiss me for a moment, my body melting into his. But as his hands wander down my backside, I pull away.

"So how was the bachelor party?" I say, staring at him.

Tucker takes a step back to meet my gaze. I think he might say something, but then he takes a step toward the refrigerator, opening it to pull out a bottle of water.

"Oh you know, same old same old with the guys. They tried everything they could to get me completely drunk, but I managed to dump a few rounds of shots into the potted plant at the corner of the bar."

I can't help but laugh. "Of course you did," I say. He sets down his water and rests his hands on the kitchen island.

"What are you still doing up? I figured you'd be passed out asleep by now."

I bite my bottom lip. I know this isn't the best time. He's obviously still drunk, and will probably get angry at what I'm about to say, but I don't have much of a choice. If I don't talk to him now, it's going to eat me alive.

"There's something I want to talk to you about."

"Okay..."

He walks around the kitchen and settles down on one of the barstools at the kitchen island. I take the seat next to him and swivel my chair until our knees are touching.

"I've been receiving some really strange messages."

"From who?"

"I don't know. The messages are from Snaptalk, so they disappear after sixty seconds."

Tucker furrows his eyebrows together. "Why are you using Snaptalk?"

"Bernie set it up for me. We like to send each other funny messages."

"Well, did you look at their profile?"

"I tried, but I couldn't find it."

Tucker takes a long drink of his water and sets it down on the countertop.

"What did the message say?"

I take a deep breath, stealing myself for what I'm about to say. I have no idea how Tucker's going to react, but I have to get this off my chest. *I have to.*

"The first message said you were a murderer. And the second that I should ask you about some little side business. And..." I find myself looking away, unable to make eye contact with him. "It said that you're not the person I think you are."

"What!? That's insane, Reese. Who would say something like that?"

I pull my gaze back to meet his. His entire posture has changed. I can see the veins popping on his neck, and the grip around his water bottle has tightened. I let out a sigh.

"I don't know who would say something like that." I raise my hands in an exasperated gesture. "It's just so weird that someone would send these messages. Why would they say those things about you?"

Tucker shakes his head. "Honestly, I have no idea. And you're certain you saw these messages? On Snaptalk?"

"Yes, why?"

The way he's looking at me suddenly makes me uncomfortable. Almost like...he doesn't believe me. Tucker must sense the shift in me, because he reaches forward and gently takes my hand. "Listen, Reese, you've been under a lot of stress lately. More than most people can handle. All of your work at the bakery, planning for the wedding... neither of us have gotten enough sleep. I just wonder if you are..."

I rip my hands away. "Are you saying I imagined those messages?"

Tucker blanches, then straightens his shoulders. "No, I just meant..." He lets his voice trail off. We sit in silence for a few seconds. Tucker runs his hands through his hair, the guilt written all over his face. Does he think I'm seeing things? I stare at him, waiting for an apology.

"The next time you get one of these messages, I want you to take a screenshot as quickly as you can and send them my way. I also want the profile information of the person that messaged you. I'll have one of my IT guys track them down. I'll get to the bottom of it."

I feel what can only be described as a wave of relief all over my body. *Of course he believes me.* I don't know why I was so afraid to bring it up to him in the first place. He's not angry at me, just at whoever sent the messages. And now he's offering to help, to get to the bottom of it. I bite my lip. I can't help feeling a little guilty I didn't go straight to him in the first place.

He leans forward and brushes a bit of hair from my face, caressing my cheek. "Is that all? Is there anything else that's bothering you?"

I chew the inside of my cheek. *There is.*

"What did the message mean by side business? Do you have a business going on besides the import-export?" I ask, trying to keep my voice steady.

Tucker shakes his head, his jaw clenching tight. "No, I don't have a 'side business,'" he says, his fingers sketching sarcastic air quotes around the words. "I run a multimillion-dollar operation where I interact with lots of different customers all over the world. And really, my work isn't anyone else's damn business."

The way he spits out those last words feels like a slap in the face, his tone dripping with condescension. My cheeks flush hot.

I take a deep breath, pushing past the sting of his words, and keep pressing for answers. "But is there anything I should know about? You know you can tell me anything, right? If there's something you're involved in..."

Tucker cuts me off with a scoff, his eyes rolling skyward in a gesture of pure exasperation. "Come on, Reese. You know me. Everything I do is on the up and up. Listen, you stick to your little bakeshop, and I'll stick to running Harding Global."

His dismissive tone feels like a punch to the gut. Suddenly I can't breathe, like all the air has been sucked out of the room.

How dare he talk to me like that?

"Little bakeshop? What is that supposed to mean?"

He lets out an exasperated sigh. "You know what I mean..."

"No, I don't. Just because my business is smaller than yours, doesn't mean it's little. And I don't appreciate you demeaning me or my bakery."

Something about the way he spoke about my bakery makes me snap. I decide to finally ask him the question that's been plaguing my mind since we started dating. *I'm tired of being left in the dark.*

"Why did you and Charlotte break up? Why won't you talk to me about it?" I feel the anger rising inside me, matching the louder tone of my voice.

"Because it doesn't matter, Reese!" He's yelling now, the anger visible on his face. "It doesn't matter what happened between me and Charlotte. You have to let it go. Move on."

"How can I when—"

Tucker reaches forward, his hand a vise around my left wrist. With a sudden yank, he pulls my hand up, forcing my engagement ring level with my eyes. The abruptness of his movement causes me to stumble slightly, my free hand bracing against the counter for balance.

His face contorts into an expression I've never seen before—a mask of anger that transforms his familiar features into something alien. It's as if a stranger has suddenly possessed him, his eyes dark and unfamiliar.

"Do you see this, Reese?" he growls. He twists my wrist slightly, making the diamond catch the light. "It means I'm marrying you, not Charlotte. It means I'm committed to you." His grip tightens further, and I can feel my pulse throbbing against his fingers. "So you need to drop all this bullshit about the past. It's over. I'm over it. And you should be too."

Tears well up in my eyes, blurring my vision. The pain in my wrist intensifies, shooting up my arm in sharp bursts. I can feel my fingers starting to tingle from restricted blood flow.

"You're hurting me," I manage to choke out.

As if snapping out of a trance, Tucker's eyes widen. "I'm sorry," he says, immediately releasing my wrist. He takes a step back, running a hand through his hair. I cradle my arm against my chest, rubbing the reddened skin where his fingers had been.

Tucker's voice softens, though there's still an edge to it. "Listen, it's been a long night. Let's just go to bed."

I watch him go, feeling as if all the air has been sucked out of the room. My body trembles slightly, adrenaline still coursing through my veins. The relief I felt earlier when he offered to investigate the Snaptalk messages for me has evaporated.

In its place is a gnawing sensation that something is very, very wrong.

CHAPTER SIXTEEN

TWO DAYS BEFORE THE WEDDING

The next morning, I roll over and reach for Tucker, but my hand meets only cold sheets. He must have left for work early and not even bothered to wake me. A dull ache begins to bloom in my chest. I sit up, the sick feeling in my stomach a sharp contrast to the bright morning light seeping through the curtains. The memory of last night's fight, the anger in Tucker's eyes when I mentioned Charlotte, makes me want to crawl back under the covers and hide.

What was I thinking, bringing her up like that? I think as I rub my eyes. I knew it was a sore spot, knew he didn't want to talk about it, especially after we ran into Amanda Spencer on the street. But I just couldn't help myself. And the way he reacted.

It was...so unlike him.

With a heavy sigh, I force myself out of bed, wincing as my bare feet hit the cold hardwood floor. I stare in the bathroom mirror. I'm not having the worst hair day, my long red tresses still carrying some of the waves I styled into them last night. But my face is puffy from the wine, and there are some dark circles under my eyes from not getting enough sleep. I splash on some makeup, and go through the motions of getting ready. But it's like I'm on autopilot, my mind a million miles away.

I glance at the clock and realize it's already seven o'clock. I'm not due into the shop until ten, as I have one last fitting for my wedding dress.

My wedding dress. The words echo in my mind, along with another thought I can't suppress: *If the wedding is still on.*

I shake my head, forcing the ridiculous thought to the back of my mind. Of course it's still on. Tucker and I just had a little fight. All couples fight, right?

My two responsibilities for the wedding were simple— find a dress and build a beautiful cake. The rest was left to the wedding planner.

Nanette's is the only wedding boutique within twenty miles of Somerville, conveniently located just a few blocks from my bakery on Main Street. It's a charming shop with pastel decor and large display windows showcasing dreamy dresses. The only catch? Nanette, the owner, is a not-so-distant cousin of Charlotte.

As I've said, escaping any connection to Charlotte seems nearly impossible in this town.

I thought about driving into Charleston, which would add about an hour to the trip, but given everything that's going on at my shop and all the other activities related to the wedding, I just didn't have time. So I had to swallow my pride and any bit of discomfort and get my dress from Nanette's.

To her credit, she never mentions Charlotte. But I always get the impression that she's on the cusp of bringing her up. She is her cousin after all, and I'm certain Charlotte came here when she was dress shopping for her wedding to Tucker.

"Reese!" she exclaims when she sees me walk in. Nanette practically runs across the room to plant two air kisses on each of my cheeks.

"How are you holding up, dear?"

"Oh, I'm fine, thank you," I say, forcing a smile.

"You look absolutely lovely," she says, her eyes appraising me from head to toe. While I appreciate the compliment, something about her tone feels disingenuous. And I know I don't look fine—dark circles like the ones I had this morning don't disappear that quickly.

"Well, your dress is ready, and I can tell you it looks absolutely fabulous. Why don't you go slip into one of the dressing rooms and I'll bring it to you."

Nanette gestures toward the silk-curtained room in the back. As I walk to the dressing room, I pass a wall adorned with photos. Gold letters proclaim, "She Said Yes to the Dress!" above a collection of about thirty images, each featuring a beaming bride in her chosen gown. I scan the pictures, wondering if any of these women ordered cakes from my bakery.

My heart stops when I spot the bottom right photo. *Charlotte.* My fiancé's ex-girlfriend, smiling radiantly in a delicate white lace gown. I squint, leaning in closer just to confirm I'm not mistaken. Why on earth would Nanette display Charlotte's photo when she never actually got married?

"Beautiful, isn't she?" Nanette's voice startles me. She's suddenly at my side, eyes fixed on Charlotte's picture. "I remember how lovely she looked in that dress. Such a shame things didn't work out."

My mouth falls open, heat quickly rising up my cheeks. She did *not* just say that. A wave of indignation washes over me, then anger. *Does everyone in this town still see Tucker as Charlotte's almost-husband? Am I just the consolation prize?* I want to scream at Nanette, demand she take down that ridiculous photo. But the words catch in my throat. This is Somerville, after all. Making a scene would only fuel the gossip mill for months.

Before I say something I might regret, I duck behind the curtain into the dressing room. My hands shake as I grip the fabric, trying to steady my breathing. I slip into the gown as quickly as I can, forcing the straps over my shoulders while swallowing my words. Once the dress is on, I take a deep breath, smoothing the material over my stomach before stepping out.

"Are you ready, dear?" Nanette chirps from the dressing area.

As soon as they see me, Nanette and her assistant gasp audibly. "Beautiful!" she says, and she clasps my shoulders, turning me until I face the mirror. I want to be angry at her, give her a piece of my mind about the photo, but as soon as I catch sight of my reflection, I stop. I'm momentarily stunned. The gown is gorgeous, hugging my curves perfectly before flowing out in a cascade of silk. My red hair, vibrant against the white fabric, completes the picture.

I feel like the bride I've always dreamed of being.

But the moment fades as my eyes drift to Charlotte's photo on the wall. Her frozen smile seems to mock me, a constant reminder of my fiancé's past. Suddenly, the beautiful dress feels suffocating. I can't shake the feeling that I'm an imposter in Charlotte's world, trying on a life that was meant to be hers.

"It's perfect," Nanette coos, but her words barely register. I nod mechanically, desperate to escape. All I want now is to get out of this dress and leave this shop. The next few minutes seem to stretch on forever while Nanette and her staff pinch and pin the dress to their satisfaction. Nanette has to step into the dressing room to help me slide off the gown, which has now been practically painted onto my skin. I barely make eye contact with Nanette as she informs me the gown will be delivered tomorrow morning.

A few minutes later, I pull open the front door of Couture Cakes and step inside. The familiar smell of the shop instantly puts me at ease. My shoulders relax back into place.

The first thing I see is a giant bouquet of white roses, magnolias, and lilies sitting near the register on the counter. The fragrance fills the room, a pleasant complement to the sugary-sweet smells of my cupcakes. I take a few quick steps and pluck the card from the bouquet.

I open the seal and pull out a small, gilded note card. I think I know whom they're from.

I just hope I'm right.

My dear Reese,

I love you more than words can say. I'm sorry about last night.
I can't wait to marry you on Saturday.

Love, Tucker.

I press the card against my chest and take a deep breath, the smell of the flowers tickling my nose. Tucker has no idea how perfect his timing is.

I have to leave the past behind. No matter how much everyone wants to remind me of Charlotte, Tucker chose me.

The mantra repeats in my head, an attempt to quell the unease that's been growing over the last few days. But it's not just about Charlotte anymore—it's about the flashes of a Tucker I don't recognize, the lingering questions about the Snaptalk messages, and the gnawing fear that I'm missing something.

Sometimes just being chosen isn't enough.

But then I look at these flowers, this thoughtful gesture, and I want to believe. I want to believe that this is the real Tucker—caring, attentive, loving. That the other moments—the anger and jealousy—are just aberrations. Stress-induced blips in an otherwise perfect relationship.

I stand there for several minutes, taking in the heady scent of flowers. When I feel like I have finally made my peace, I tuck the card into my pocket to make my way around the counter. I busy myself pulling some cupcakes from the back cooler and placing them in our display. We mostly sell our pastries in bulk to local customers and companies, but I always love having a full display out front to showcase our selection.

When the bell from the front door jingles, I turn on my heel, ready to greet one of my customers with a smile. My elation over the apology flowers suddenly falls flat.

Monica Harding is walking in the door. And even though she's wearing that sickly sweet smile, I know she's not here for anything good.

CHAPTER SEVENTEEN

"Good morning, Reese, my dear," Monica says, her heels clicking on the hardwood floor as she walks over to the counter and air-kisses me on both cheeks. Her perfume, a mix of gardenias and spice, fills my nostrils, making me feel slightly lightheaded. She's dressed to the nines as usual, in a fitted baby-blue suit that perfectly matches her designer handbag. Her dark hair is swept up in a loose chignon, with a few artfully curled tendrils framing her face.

"These are absolutely stunning," she says, leaning in to smell the bouquet of roses and peonies on the counter. She closes her eyes for a moment, inhaling deeply, before returning her sharp gaze to mine.

"Thank you, Monica," I say, trying to keep my voice light and even.

"Really quite lovely," she continues, her fingers brushing delicately over the velvety petals. "Are these from Tucker? Or Zach?"

My stomach drops, and a sickly feeling tightens around

my chest. *Did she just say Zach?* I think, panic rising in my throat like bile.

"From Tucker," I manage, my voice sounding strained to my own ears.

"Oh." She arches an eyebrow, her lips curving into a knowing smirk. "These look like apology flowers. Did you two have a fight last night?"

I want to brush off her comment, to laugh and tell her she's being ridiculous. But the way her eyes are boring into mine, sharp and probing, makes me feel like a naughty child caught with her hand in the cookie jar.

"Oh, you know, just a little pre-wedding disagreement over some details. We're so excited about the big day." My voice sounds tense, awkward. I swallow hard, trying to moisten my dry mouth. "What can I do for you, Monica? Is there something you need for the wedding?"

"Oh, well, I was just checking in on you." Monica's eyes narrow slightly. "You know, to see how you were doing. The wedding is just a few days away. The week of my own wedding, I was just a mess."

I find this hard to believe. But I paint a smile on my face as she continues.

"It was an incredible amount of pressure. I started to make some questionable decisions."

The way she enunciates "questionable decisions" makes my stomach bunch up in knots. She's going somewhere with this, and I know I'm not going to like it. I clear my throat.

"Oh, well, you know, I'm doing fine. I just had my dress fitting and it went really well. The dress is gorgeous. But I am looking forward to getting the wedding over with, so Tucker and I can start enjoying our life together."

"You're not enjoying it now?"

"I just meant—"

"Well, I admire your grace under pressure, Reese," she says, absently fingering a magnolia pedal. "By the way, I saw you the other day at Marla's with Zach. You two looked pretty cozy."

Oh, here we go. That familiar heat crawls up the sides of my cheeks.

"Oh, Zach? He's just been working with me on the museum gala. He's actually in charge of running the event this year and I've been working with him on the catering."

"Yes, I heard. *Under the Sea* is the theme for this year. I had an invitation, but of course I'll be at a wedding this Saturday."

The way she says it...it takes everything in me not to shove her right out of my shop. But I pull together a tight smile.

"Yes. As you can see"—I point to the table inside the tasting room full of decorated pastries—"I've been working all week to get these finished." I breathe in through my nose. *Maybe leveling with her is the best approach.* "You don't have anything to worry about, Monica. There's nothing going on with me and Zach. That's all in the past."

"Of course, of course," Monica says, waving her hand. "Tucker knows about you and Zach working together, right?"

The heat in my cheeks intensifies. "Yes—I mean, no—" I'm stammering now.

Pull it together, Reese.

"I haven't told him about it. I mean, he knows about the gala, but he doesn't know that Zach and I are working together."

She pulls off a petal from one of the flowers and rolls it between her fingertips before dropping it on the counter. I watch her, frozen where I'm standing. She pulls her head back and looks down her nose at me.

"You tell Tucker that you've been working with Zach, or I'll have to do it for you. Walking down the aisle with a secret between the two of you is no way to start a marriage." She pauses. "Tucker is my cousin. We grew up together. He's practically my brother. If I get wind that you're sneaking around behind his back with your ex-boyfriend? After what he's been through?" She narrows her eyes at me. "I'll make sure you never do business in this town."

I can feel the blood pulsing behind my eyes as I try to process her audacity. I'm so completely shocked by her open threat that my mouth drops open of its own accord. It takes everything in me not to reach over the counter and grab the lapels of her tailored suit.

How dare she...

"As I told you before, Monica, you have nothing to worry about."

She leans back, as if appraising me. "You have until tomorrow morning before I tell Tucker myself," she says with an air of finality. Just as I open my mouth to respond, Bernie emerges from the back of the shop. Her presence suddenly breaks the tension in the room. I force myself to let out a breath and take a step back.

"Monica, how lovely to see you," Bernie greets her with a smile.

"Hello, Bernie," Monica responds, her eyes darting between the two of us. "I should be on my way now."

With a dramatic turn on her heel, she turns and clicks her heels out of the room. The tension lingers in the air even after she's gone, leaving me reeling.

"What was that all about?" Bernie asks.

"What?" I turn to her, my cheeks still hot. "Oh, it was nothing, Monica was just complaining about the seating arrangement at the reception. You know how particular she is..."

"I've heard," she says, rolling her eyes. "Listen, I have a few errands to run this afternoon. Do you mind if I leave a little early?"

"Of course not. Go ahead, no problem."

"Thanks," she says, then disappears back into the shop.

After Bernie is gone, I find myself alone in the stillness of the bakery, my thoughts spinning so fast it makes me dizzy. I can't shake the image of Monica's face as she left, the way her eyes had flashed with a mixture of triumph and warning.

I hate to admit it, but she's right.

I need to tell Tucker about Zach. I was just planning on telling him after the wedding. I knew he would be annoyed, maybe even angry, but I would assure him he had nothing to worry about. But now, with Monica's warning ringing in my ears and the pressure of my own guilt, I know that I can't wait. I have to lay all my cards on the table, tell him everything. *I just hope he understands.*

CHAPTER EIGHTEEN

I close the shop early, having finished all the preparations for the gala. I've laid the last of the finished pastries to rest in the walk-in cooler, awaiting delivery on Saturday. Before leaving, I send a message to Tucker, informing him of my plans to make a steak dinner tonight. Though I'm a baker by trade, I can whip up a delicious meal when I put my mind to it. I stop by the market, gathering an array of ingredients for Tucker's dinner, not forgetting to pick up a couple of extra bottles of wine and his favorite bourbon. Any conversation is better with a full belly and a few glasses of wine, so I'm hoping a nice steak dinner will soften the blow.

A headache is brewing in my mind, the magnitude of the conversation we're about to have pressing down on me like a ton of bricks. Tucker has always been the jealous type, a trait I once found endearing. Knowing that, I never should have divulged the fact that I dated Zach, much less that we *slept* together. This revelation only complicates matters, even though Zach and I are merely friends now. Whenever someone mentions Zach at a party or gathering—or worse, when the three of us attend the same event—Tucker becomes extremely irritable. We usually end up going home early.

If Tucker discovers that I've been working with Zach without telling him? He will be furious. I've already accepted that. In fact, if we weren't mere days away from our wedding, it might be grounds for a breakup. But I know Tucker well enough to know that he'll never call off the wedding, not after what happened with Charlotte. Not with all his work colleagues, friends, and family flying into town to watch him walk down the aisle, *again*.

There's simply too much at stake for him.

Knowing this brings me some comfort, but it also fills me with immense guilt. I know I am being unfair to Tucker. I had intended to tell him about Zach after the wedding, but Monica's ultimatum has forced my hand.

But what if Tucker can't forgive me?

A cold, unsettling feeling grips my stomach. I have to take a deep breath to steady myself. *I can't think like that.* Tucker loves me, and I love him. Forgiveness is part of the pact. I've made a mistake, an error in judgment. It's not the end of the world.

But even as I try to cling to that certainty, I can't shake the nagging voice in the back of my mind, the one that whispers that I've made a terrible mistake. That by keeping Zach a secret, by letting him into my life in a way that I knew Tucker wouldn't approve of, I've jeopardized everything that matters to me.

I pour myself a glass of wine and put on soft piano music, trying to calm myself. When I hear the rumbling of the garage door opening, I know Tucker has arrived. He enters the room, looking slightly tired, his movements slow and deliberate.

"It smells fantastic in here."

He doesn't waste any time crossing the room and wrapping me up in his arms. He gives me a long kiss, and I can smell the faint hint of his aftershave. Something about his embrace always makes me melt a bit inside.

"Thank you for the flowers you sent today," I say.

He pulls away from me and cups my shoulders in his hands while looking into my eyes. "I love you so much, Reese, and I don't want anything to come between us."

"Me too," I say quietly. *We're about to put that to the test.*

He makes himself busy pulling out a wine goblet from the cabinet and pouring himself a drink, and then he settles in at the kitchen island to watch me work. After a few moments, he raises his glass.

"Here's to us," he says.

"To us," I say, tapping my glass against his. "So, how was your day? Anything exciting happening at work?"

He lets out a long sigh. "Oh, you know I'm just trying to wrap up a couple deals before the wedding this weekend. I've got a few customers coming into town who I'm excited for you to meet. They are real characters."

I've met a few of Tucker's clients before, and "characters" is a great way of putting it. Are these guys sketchy? It's hard to say for sure. On the surface, they all seem to be legitimate businessmen, with thriving companies and impressive portfolios. But there's something about the way they carry themselves, the way they exchange loaded glances, that makes me wonder.

Either way, it's Tucker's business, not mine.

"I'm sure I'm in for a treat."

I take a step across the kitchen. "Speaking of treats..." I open up the oven. A blast of warm air comes out, practically melting my mascara. I reach in and pull out a tray of freshly baked crab cakes. Using a spatula, I pull one off the tray and settle it onto a plate with a sprig of parsley. I pick up the plate and slide it in front of Tucker. "I made your favorite crab cakes."

"You're too good to me," he says, flashing me a smile.

"Dinner will be ready in about twenty minutes," I say. "You can hang out here with me or take a shower if you like."

It only takes a few forkfuls for him to devour the food. He scrapes up the last few bits of his crab cake and wipes his mouth with a napkin before answering. "I'll shower."

On his way out of the kitchen he comes around the counter to give me another kiss, this time on my neck. It sends a jolt of anticipation through me. Tucker has a way of just turning me on in general. I suppose it's one of the things that keeps us together. "The heat between the sheets," as they say.

I make myself busy, searing the steaks before popping them into the oven. I blanch some asparagus on the top of the stove. My phone, which I have placed on silent mode, begins to buzz. I look over to see who's calling and don't recognize the number, so I decide to ignore it. The last thing I need is a distraction right now, or another cryptic message. I need to finish dinner with Tucker and tell him the truth about Zach. Nothing is more important.

The wine is working its way through my bloodstream, relaxing me and giving me a little bit of a buzz. Just as I'm about ready to drop the asparagus onto a serving platter my phone buzzes again. I let out a deep sigh.

Who could be calling me right now? What do they want?

Again, I dismiss the call and let it go to voicemail. A few minutes later I have everything prepared and ready to go. I'm plating the dishes and taking them into the dining room for us to have dinner when Tucker appears in the kitchen, the faint smell of his spiced soap filling the room as he walks in. He gives me a kiss on the cheek and goes to fill up his wine glass.

My phone starts buzzing. Again, I ignore it.

"Do you need to get that?"

I let out a sigh, glaring at the phone while it purrs on the table.

"Oh no, it's probably just a spam caller."

Buzz...

"I think you should answer it. It might be urgent."

Fine. Balancing a wine glass in one hand I reach over and swipe over the phone.

"Hello?" I say, my voice sounding a bit harsh.

"Is this Reese Montgomery? The owner of Couture Cakes?" The voice is of a man, his tone slightly raspy.

"Yes?"

"Miss Montgomery, this is Lieutenant Connors with the Somerville police department. I'm afraid there's been a burglary at your shop."

I set down my wine glass, all of the blood in my veins turning ice cold.

"Okay..."

"We'd like you to meet us here right away. Is that possible?"

"Yes," I say, my voice quivering like a leaf. "I can be there in fifteen minutes."

"See you then," he says and hangs up the phone.

I look up at Tucker, who's staring at me. My legs feel

suddenly week and I grip the side of the kitchen island to steady myself.

"What happened?"

"Someone's broken into the shop," I say, mustering all the strength I have not to burst into tears. He doesn't hesitate, reaching out for his keys.

"I'll drive," he says.

Looks like the conversation about Zach will have to wait.

CHAPTER NINETEEN

The drive to the shop is a tense and silent blur, my hands clammy with sweat as I nervously rub them together. Tucker's jaw is clenched tight and his eyes remain fixed on the road ahead. He doesn't attempt to make small talk, which is probably for the best. I'm afraid that if I open my mouth, I'll break down in tears. I manage to steady my hands long enough to send Bernie a text, updating her on the situation and promising to keep her informed.

How could this happen?

I haven't invested much in the shop's security system, only installing a camera out front, mainly for show. It's not hooked up to any monitoring service. After all, this is Somerville, a place where people leave their cars unlocked and set their purses on the counter while shopping. Crime is rare here, especially on Main Street, where Couture Cakes and a string of quaint little shops are located. In this community, people keep an eye out for each other and if anything strange happens, everyone knows about it.

I never keep cash on hand in the shop; all of our transactions are done through credit card. The most valuable items in the shop are my baking equipment, but I doubt there's a high demand for an industrial stand mixer on the resale market.

So why would someone break into my shop now?

As our car pulls up to the curb, my heart pounds against my chest like a drum. Police cars, their red and blue lights flashing in the late-night haze, line the street. We come to a stop in front of the shop and my eyes struggle to process what I'm seeing.

In bright, hot pink spray paint, words are scrawled across the front of the building. "Slut. Whore." The letters are jagged and crude, dripping down the windows and smearing across the display cases.

A wave of nausea washes over me, threatening to overwhelm me completely. *Who could have done this?* My mind flashes back to the strange messages I've been receiving from Snaptalk... Is there a connection?

Tucker parks the car and runs over to open the door for me. He grabs my hand and holds it firmly as the two of us walk up to the front of the shop to assess the damage. My legs are shaking so badly I can barely stand. While the two large display windows have been vandalized with spray paint, the glass on the front door of the shop has been completely shattered. It looks as though someone broke the glass and then chipped it away so they could walk through.

Tucker leads me toward the door, careful not to tread on any glass. The two of us step inside where a handful of police officers are waiting. They're all dressed in uniform, a couple of them chatting on one side of the room while the other three are taking photos and notes of the space.

A man suddenly appears in front of me, reaching out to shake my hand. "Miss Montgomery? I'm Lieutenant Connors. I called you earlier."

"Yes, I'm Reese Montgomery," I say, my voice sounding feeble and weak. "This is my fiancé, Tucker Harding." The two men shake hands.

"It's nice to meet you both. I'm sorry it's under these circumstances. We got an anonymous call about an hour ago. The caller said they heard glass breaking and then saw someone with a flashlight walking around the shop."

He keeps talking, discussing the extent of the damage. I'm trying my best to pay attention and nod along, but all I can focus on is the chaotic state of the shop.

My eyes bounce around the room, taking in every detail. The overturned chair in the corner, the broken dome of the display case, shattered glass scattered across the floor, glinting under the flickering fluorescent lights. Deep scratches mar the once pristine wallpaper, its delicate floral pattern now interrupted by jagged, angry lines. The pastry counter, once a showcase of baked treats, now lies in ruins, its contents strewn haphazardly across the tile. Shards of porcelain from smashed teacups crunch underfoot as I step further into the chaos.

The carefully crafted ambiance of the quaint bakery has been shattered.

And so has my heart.

My eyes burn with impending tears. I'm afraid if I start crying now I'll never stop. I give myself permission to sob into my pillow later, because it's not going to help me here. For now I can only think of one place I need to see—the walk-in cooler that holds all of the pastries for the gala. And, of course, *my wedding cake*. With both events only a couple of days away, if they are destroyed, I don't know what I'll do.

"I'll be right back," I whisper to Tucker, who is discussing the details of the situation with Lieutenant Connors.

I rush around the broken display counter and move past my office and into the kitchen with my heart in my throat. When I reach the back, my hands gently grasp the heavy stainless steel door to the walk-in cooler and pull. It doesn't budge.

It's still locked. I let out a huge sigh of relief. We usually lock up at the end of the day and thankfully, Bernie didn't forget. I quickly retrace my steps back to my office and retrieve the keys. When I finally open the door, I practically scream out with joy.

Everything for the gala is still carefully stored, and standing in the middle is my wedding cake.

It's stunning. The cake stands tall and graceful, its three tiers covered in a flawless, smooth white fondant. Delicate, shimmering pearls are meticulously arranged in intricate patterns, spiraling around each tier in perfect asymmetry. The pearls catch the light, creating a subtle glow. It literally takes my breath away.

Bernie has truly outdone herself, creating exactly what I had pictured in my mind's eye. Actually, no, it's even *better*.

I give myself a moment to stand there and admire it. Then I take three deep, calming breaths. The front of the shop may be a mess, but at least the events for the weekend are locked up safe. When I'm done, I make sure to relock the door before heading back out front.

The police officers are gone, their flashing lights fading

into the distance as I watch the last car pulling away on the street. The once chaotic scene has settled into an unsettling silence. Tucker stands in the middle of the vandalized shop, his phone pressed to his ear.

I walk up next to him, my footsteps echoing in the empty space, and he instinctively wraps his arm around my shoulders, pulling me close. His touch is comforting, a reminder that I'm not alone. As he speaks into the phone, his words are clear and decisive.

"Yes, I need a team here right away," he says, his voice steady and unwavering. "Bring paint thinner, a scraper, whatever you think you'll need from the warehouse for the windows, plus cleaning supplies and bags. I want at least four guys on this. I need it gone by morning."

He pauses, listening to the response on the other end of the line, before continuing with instructions about plywood for the front door.

As I stand there, leaning into his embrace, my heart swells with gratefulness for my fiancé. I've always prided myself on being an independent woman, not a girl that needs rescuing, but right now, in the face of this mess, I'll gladly accept his help and support.

He wraps up the call and slides his phone back into his pocket.

"I've got my night shift manager on his way, with part of my maintenance team. They will remove the paint from the windows, clean and repair what they can, and secure the front door." He strokes my hair. "I don't want you to worry about a thing."

"Thank you," I whisper as I lean into his warm body, a small sense of peace washing over me.

"Reese?"

The sound of my name, spoken in that achingly familiar tone, sends a wave of unease through my body. I pull away from Tucker, my heart pounding in my chest as I turn toward the front door, toward the direction of the voice.

Because there, standing in the doorway, is Zach.

CHAPTER TWENTY

I take a deep breath, my heart pounding in my chest as I step forward, placing myself between Zach and Tucker. "Zach," I say, my voice trembling slightly as I swallow hard, my mouth suddenly dry. "What are you doing here?"

Zach shifts his weight from one foot to the other, his hands shoved deep into his pockets. He scans the vandalized bakery before his eyes meet mine. "My cousin Jake works for the police department. He said there was a break-in on Main Street at the bakery. I came to see if you needed any help."

I glance back at Tucker, who stands behind me, his arms crossed over his chest, jaw clenched, and eyes flashing with anger. The heat of his gaze is almost palpable.

"We don't need your help," Tucker says, his voice low and dangerous, each word dripping with barely contained rage.

Zach raises an eyebrow, his eyes sweeping over the destruction that surrounds us. "Are you sure?" he asks, his tone laced with concern. "It's a mess in here."

"I've already taken care of it, but thanks, man," he says, his words clipped.

I turn back to Zach, my hands clasped tightly in front of me. "Zach, thank you for coming," I say, keeping my voice steady. "Tucker's got a team on the way that's going to clean everything out by morning."

Zach takes a step closer to me, his eyes searching mine as he lowers his voice. "Do you know who did this?"

"No," I say quickly, cutting him off before he can press further. I avert my eyes, not wanting to delve into the details of the break-in, especially not with Zach.

Zach nods slowly. "Okay, I get it. But Reese, if you need anything, just call me, all right?" He reaches out as if to touch my arm, but thinks better of it, letting his hand fall back to his side.

"She won't be calling you, Zach. I don't know what your game is, but you need to back off," Tucker growls, taking another step forward, his fists clenched at his sides. "Reese is my fiancée, and I don't need you sniffing around here like some lovesick puppy."

I take a deep breath, trying to find the right words to defuse the situation, but my mind is spinning. I open my mouth to defend Zach and explain he's just a friend, but Tucker is striding toward him with his shoulders squared for fight. Zach's eyes flash with anger, his own posture stiffening in response

"Listen, Tucker, you need to chill out. We're just friends, okay? The only time we ever see each other is when we're working on the gala."

Tucker's eyes narrow, his brow furrowing in confusion and suspicion. He turns to me, his face intense and questioning. "What do you mean, working on the gala?"

My stomach rumbles, and I suddenly feel the need to throw up. A wave of nausea washes over me. *Oh no.* This is not the way I had planned on telling Tucker about Zach and the gala.

I take a deep breath, trying to steady myself as I look Tucker in the eyes. "Zach was the one who got me the job at the gala. We had a couple of meetings to go over the pastries," I say, my voice trembling slightly.

Tucker's expression hardens, his jaw clenching as he takes a few steps back. He turns to face me, his eyes flashing with a mixture of hurt and anger. "You were working with him," he says, pointing accusingly at Zach, his voice rising with each word, "and you didn't tell me about it?"

I can see Tucker's cheeks flush, the color rising in his face as his anger builds.

I'm in trouble.

My mind spins, desperately trying to think of a way to get Zach out of the shop before the situation escalates further. I take a few steps toward Zach, giving him a pointed look, silently pleading for him to understand.

"Zach, I'll have Bernie call you tomorrow and let you know about the gala delivery. But everything is safely locked in the cooler, so we're all good to go," I say, my words rushed and clipped. "Thank you for coming, but I think you should go."

Zach nods, his expression a mix of concern and understanding. He takes a step back, his hands still raised in a gesture of surrender. "I'm glad everything is okay, Reese. I'll talk to you tomorrow," he says, his voice calm and measured.

He turns to Tucker, giving him a tense nod, then walks out the door.

The moment he's gone, I feel the weight of Tucker's gaze

on me. The vandalized bakery suddenly feels claustrophobic, the walls closing in around us. I take a deep breath, steeling myself for the inevitable confrontation, knowing that the truth about Zach and the gala can no longer be avoided.

Tucker rounds on me, his eyes blazing. "When were you going to tell me that you've been working with Zach on the gala? When were you going to let me know that you've been sneaking around behind my back with your ex-boyfriend!?"

It's as though I've been slapped, my cheeks burning with shame and indignation. "I haven't been sneaking around!" I protest, my voice cracking with tears. "Zach is just a friend, Tucker. He's been helping me with the gala, that's all. There's nothing going on between us."

But even as the words leave my lips, I know they're not entirely accurate. Because the truth is, you always leave a piece of yourself with someone you've dated. It's like an invisible thread connecting you to your past. And with Zach, that connection runs deeper. We shared not just emotions, but physical intimacy. It's a bond that lingers, even after the relationship is over.

I glance at Tucker, seeing the tightness around his eyes. He understands this unspoken reality too.

"I'm sorry," I whisper, the words feeling woefully inadequate. "I should have told you about Zach, about the gala. I never meant to hurt you, Tucker. I swear it."

"But you did hurt me, Reese. You lied to me, made me feel like an idiot. How am I supposed to trust you after this?"

Tears begin to well up in my eyes, hot and stinging. "I know. I know I messed up. But please, Tucker, you have to believe me. There's nothing going on between me and Zach. He's just a friend, someone who's been helping me with the gala. That's all."

"And what about the messages, huh? The vandalism? You think that's just a coincidence?"

"What do you mean is it just a coincidence?

Tucker raises both eyebrows at me, waiting for the puzzle pieces to come together. *He couldn't mean...*

"You think Zach did this?"

"It kind of makes sense, doesn't it? He obviously doesn't want us to be together. And so he's doing everything he can to stop the wedding."

I shake my head. "No way. If he didn't want me to marry you, he would just tell me. And he hasn't told me that. It's quite the opposite. Zach is my friend and he's happy for me."

"You're being naïve, Reese."

I shift my weight, feeling like I'm grasping at straws. "I don't know who's doing this, Tucker, but I swear to you it has nothing to do with Zach. He wouldn't do anything like that."

He looks at me then, his eyes dark. "I want to believe you, Reese. God knows I do. But right now, I don't know what to think. I don't know who to trust."

I nod, feeling the gravitas of his words like a physical blow. "I understand. And I know I have a lot to make up for. But please, Tucker, don't give up on me. Don't give up on us." I take a step closer to him, placing my hand on his arm. "I love you, and I'll do whatever it takes to earn back your trust."

He sighs. "I love you too, Reese. But right now, I think I just need some space."

I swallow hard, feeling like my heart is breaking in two.

"Okay," I whisper, my voice barely audible over the pounding of my own heart. "I understand."

"My guys will be here in a few minutes. Take my car and go home. We'll talk in the morning."

I open my mouth to protest, but before I can utter a sound, Tucker slaps the keys into my hand, the metal biting into my skin. The magnitude of everything unspoken between us hangs in the air. Even if we did start hashing it out right now, I have no idea what I would say. So, with my head bowed, I stumble out the broken front door.

CHAPTER TWENTY-ONE

My feet carry me to the driver's seat of the car as if on autopilot. The ride home passes in a blur, the streets and lights melding together in a hazy kaleidoscope of emotions. My mind keeps flashing back to the scene at the shop, the ugly words spray-painted across the windows, the shattered glass littering the sidewalk. It's like a nightmare come to life, a violation of the one place that has always been my sanctuary. Even worse than the physical damage are the questions.

Who would write these things? And why?

And I only made matters worse by keeping secrets from Tucker. We could have faced the strange and threatening messages together, but by allowing myself to stay in touch with Zach, I've broken the trust that we've worked so hard to build.

Tucker was so eager to help, to shield me from the pain of my destroyed shop. He was so calm, so stable. *And what have I done in return?* I've lied to him, hidden things from him, made him feel like a fool. The guilt is like a physical force on my chest, pressing down until I can barely breathe. I crack the window of the car, looking for any respite from the panic.

As for who broke into the shop? *I have no idea.*

I swerve suddenly, realizing I've let the car venture over the center line. I've got to focus on my driving. I unbutton my shirt, trying to let some of the heat escape my body. When the front gates of our home finally slide into view, the tears start coming. There's nothing else I can do. I stop the car in front of the house and start sobbing. This is not where I saw myself just days from my dream wedding, sobbing uncontrollably in my fiancé's car while he puts the pieces of my shop back together. After a few minutes of letting the tears flow, a new question punches me in the stomach.

For the second time in two days, a singular thought jumps into my head: *Is the wedding even still on?* Honestly, I have no idea. I can only hope that Tucker will forgive me. Monica was right, *painfully* right, that starting off a marriage with a lie is no way to go. Even if it's a little white lie like omitting the fact that I was working with on the gala with my ex-boyfriend.

As I pull the car into the garage, a sense of dread washes over me. I try some deep calming breaths, but that just makes me start crying again. I finally make it inside, my footsteps echoing hollowly on the hardwood floors. The house feels cold and empty, like all the warmth has been sucked out of it.

The faint smell of dinner still hangs in the air, reminding me of my failed plans. I force my body to keep moving, dumping the now spoiled food in the trash and cleaning up the kitchen on autopilot. I scrub the kitchen from top to bottom, my hands raw and aching. I listen desperately for any sound of Tucker, the creak of the door announcing his return.

He doesn't.

When there is nothing left to do, I turn and head upstairs. My steps are heavy, like I have a brick strapped to each foot. The adrenaline from earlier has subsided and exhaustion is settling over me. I head into the bathroom, my footsteps echoing off the polished marble floors.

As I wash away the last traces of my makeup, I catch a glimpse of my reflection in the ornate, gilt-framed mirror. My face looks drawn and tired, the events of the day etched into the lines around my eyes and the tightness of my jaw.

Just as I'm reaching for my toothbrush, my phone buzzes insistently on the countertop. I hesitate for a moment, tempted to ignore it, to lose myself in the mundane comfort of my bedtime rituals. But I know I can't ignore it. Besides, what if it's Tucker calling to tell me everything's okay?

With a sigh, I pick up the phone and swipe through the messages. The first is from Bernie.

> How is the shop? What did the police say?

I quickly text her back, assuring her that the cleanup is underway and that none of the other pastries were damaged. But I can't bring myself to tell her about the vicious graffiti that was sprayed across the glass, the ugly words that scarred our charming little shop. As I swipe to the next message, this one on Snaptalk, my heart nearly stops. It's from an unknown number, the text glowing ominously on the screen.

> *Hope you enjoyed the new decorations to your shop. That's just a taste of what's to come if you don't call off the wedding. You have two days left.*

My fingers shake as I try to capture a screenshot, but before I can even blink, the message vanishes into the ether, leaving no trace of its existence.

I sink down onto the plush bed, my mind reeling with the implications. Someone out there hates me, wants to destroy my life, my happiness, my future with Tucker. But why?

At this point, I don't have much energy left to worry about it. Exhaustion finally claims me, and I collapse into bed, my clothes still on, pressing down upon me like a physical manifestation of my guilt. I slide underneath the covers, feeling the cool sheets wrap around my body. As sleep tugs at the edges of my consciousness, one final, haunting thought echoes through my mind.

Who would want to ruin my wedding?

CHAPTER TWENTY-TWO

ONE DAY BEFORE THE WEDDING

The next morning, I wake up and instinctively glance over to the spot where Tucker should be lying beside me. The bed is empty. A pang of disappointment hits me in the chest. I run my fingers over the smooth sheets, feeling their softness. I vaguely remember Tucker coming in last night and crawling into bed next to me.

But now he's gone.

The fact that Tucker has already left for the day without even saying a word to me is not a promising sign. I drag myself out of bed and head to the bathroom, trying to compose myself as I apply some makeup and change into a comfortable lounge outfit before heading downstairs.

When I walk into the kitchen, relief floods over my body. Tucker is there with a dish towel hanging over his shoulder while he makes scrambled eggs and bacon. There is a full pot of coffee, and a couple of mugs are sitting on the counter. It's been months since he made me breakfast. I take it as a sign he's ready to talk, at the very least.

"Good morning," he says, glancing up as I enter the

room. His voice is soft, tinged with a wariness that mirrors my own.

"Morning," I reply, settling onto one of the high-backed stools at the kitchen island. The marble countertop is cool beneath my fingertips, a stark contrast to the steaming mug of coffee Tucker sets before me. For a moment, we simply sit in silence, the only sounds the distant chirping of birds in the sprawling magnolia trees outside. It's a far cry from the laughter and easy banter that usually fills our mornings.

Finally, Tucker clears his throat, his gaze meeting mine with a mixture of emotions I don't recognize. "I know we need to talk," he says, "and I thought it would be best if we did it over breakfast."

I nod, my stomach growling involuntarily at the mention of food. In the chaos of the previous evening, I had foregone dinner, too consumed with worry and guilt to even think about eating.

"I agree," I say, my voice sounding small and uncertain to my own ears. "There's so much we need to discuss, so much I need to apologize for."

I take a sip of my coffee, the rich, bold flavor bursting on my tongue and bringing a momentary clarity to my sleep-fogged brain. *Where do I even begin?* I wonder, my heart clenching at the thought of the difficult conversation ahead.

"I wish you would have told me about Zach," Tucker says, his tone more weary than accusatory. Still, the words hit me like a punch to the gut, a stark reminder of my own thoughtlessness.

"I am so sorry, Tucker," I breathe, my eyes filling with tears. "I didn't want to upset you, and I didn't think it was a big deal. Zach and I are just friends." Even as the words leave my lips, I know how hollow they sound.

"It's a big deal to me," he says quietly, his gaze boring into mine with an intensity that takes my breath away. "Can you understand that, Reese? Can you see how much it hurts to know that you kept this from me, that you didn't trust me enough to be honest about your relationship with Zach?"

I nod, shame and regret washing over me. "I do understand," I whisper, my voice cracking. "And I'm so sorry, Tucker. I never meant to hurt you or make you doubt my love for you."

I reach across the countertop, my hand finding his and holding on tight. "Can you forgive me?" I ask, my heart in my throat as I search his face.

For a long moment, he simply looks at me, his expression unreadable. And then, just when I'm sure that all is lost, he sighs, his fingers tightening around mine in a gesture of reassurance.

"Of course I forgive you. I love you."

I let out a breath I didn't even know I was holding. Something bubbles up inside of me: *hope*. If we could get through this? Maybe we can just get through the wedding too.

"It's just...all the stress from the wedding, the strange text messages, everyone talking about Charlotte," I say, noticing Tucker's face tighten at the mention of her name. I push on, "I wanted to tell you about working with Zach...but the timing never felt right."

He gives me a pained look. "But you could have told me from the beginning, when he approached you about the job."

I've really messed up, I think, my stomach churning with guilt.

"I know. It was wrong of me. I promise it will never happen again." Tucker takes a few bites of his breakfast, chewing in silence. I follow suit, the greasy bacon and scrambled eggs warming my belly and providing some comfort.

"Tonight's the rehearsal dinner," Tucker says, breaking the silence. "Everyone who's coming to the wedding is arriving today. We have a big day ahead of us. Let's just put this behind us, okay?"

As Tucker speaks of leaving the past behind us, my mind inevitably drifts to Charlotte. I've laid all my cards on the table now—he knows about Zach and the messages. Yet, the mystery of his breakup with Charlotte remains unspoken, a shadow lingering at the edges of our relationship.

The question burns on the tip of my tongue: *What really happened between you and Charlotte?* But I can't bring myself to voice it. He's forgiven my lie about Zach, and I'm acutely aware of how fragile our reconciliation feels. It's as if we're balancing on a tightrope, and one misstep—one more mention of Charlotte—could send us plummeting, destroying everything we've built.

So I swallow all my questions and reach out across the table and hold his hand.

"I love you," I say.

"I love you too," he replies, his tone softer. I slide out of my seat and make my way around the corner, wrapping my arms around his waist.

"Thank you for giving me another chance," I whisper, my face pressed against his back.

Tucker doesn't respond, but he turns in my embrace, his lips finding mine in a deep kiss. I lose myself in the moment, his hands roaming over my body. Before I know it, he's pulling off my shirt, his fingers skimming over my bare skin. Making love on the cold tile floor wasn't what I had in mind, but at this point, I'll do anything to show Tucker how much I love him.

CHAPTER TWENTY-THREE

An hour later, the two of us are showered and ready to head out the door. Tucker gives me one last lingering kiss before jumping in his car to head to the office. The scent of his cologne and the warmth of his embrace still linger on my skin. I can't deny that the make-up sex was amazing, passionate and intense, but it still feels like the truce between us is tenuous at best.

Tucker finding out I was working with Zach has broken his trust, and it'll take more than just some steamy make-up sex to fix that. The betrayal in his eyes when he confronted me about it still haunts me. But the wedding is moving forward, so I suppose I have the rest of my life to make it up to him.

Driving to the shop now, a sickening twist in my stomach makes me feel like I might lose my breakfast at any moment. My dream, my perfect little bakery, *vandalized*. The memory of the shattered glass and cruel words spray-painted on the window flashes through my mind, again and again. I am still trying to understand why someone would do this to me.

Zach was right. Charlotte doesn't really have a motive; she was the one who left Tucker, after all. But I'm just not sure who else would be so angry that they would destroy everything or write those words on the shop door.

When Tucker and I started dating, he was single, free, and clear. Charlotte had left him at the altar, and he wasn't seeing anybody else. In fact, I was the one who was seeing someone at the time. But Zach and I ended things amicably, and we're still friends.

So again, who would do this to me?

As I pull up to the shop, I see that Bernie is already there. She's made progress on cleaning up the front counter, rearranging the furniture back into its place, and for the most part, the shop looks normal. I'll need to redo the wallpaper at some point, but I can worry about that after this weekend.

The warm, inviting scent of freshly baked pastries fills the air, replacing the lingering odor of spray paint and disinfectants. The only real remaining reminder of what happened last night is the plywood on the front door. Tucker's team did a fantastic job cleaning up the glass. Honestly, the glass looks cleaner today than it did yesterday, sparkling in the morning sunlight.

"Bernie," I say as I enter the back room. She is bent over a tray of cupcakes, carefully piping a dollop of icing on each one. I asked her to come in early and get an early start on replacing the items in the display case. "Thank you so much for coming in early to help."

"Of course," she says. There is an awkward pause while Bernie looks at me, gripping the bag of icing in her hand. She swallows. "Do you know who did this?"

"Honestly, I have no idea." And really, *that's the truth.* I have theories, yes. But do I really know who wants me to cancel the wedding? Who is threatening me if I don't? Regardless, I need to give Bernie something to ease her concern.

"I think it might be some local kids just doing vandalism in the area."

Bernie puts down the piping bag, and her face hardens. "I'd like to give those kids a piece of my mind."

"Me too, Bernie," I say, forcing a weak smile.

We spend the next couple of hours tidying up the shop, restocking the display and wiping down the countertops until they gleam. I gratefully lose myself in the mundane tasks of putting the shop back together.

Finally, as we finish putting away the last of the cleaning supplies, I remember to tell Bernie what I found last night in the walk-in cooler. I walk over and gently touch her shoulder. "Bernie," I say softly, "I saw the wedding cake last night. It's absolutely stunning. Everything I could have ever dreamed of."

A faint blush creeps into Bernie's cheeks, and she ducks her head shyly. "Really? You like it?"

"It's exactly what I was hoping for. Thank you, thank you," I say, pulling her into an awkward hug. Bernie stiffens for a moment, unused to such displays of affection, but then tentatively pats my back.

As we pull apart, I glance at the clock on the wall and feel a jolt of panic. It's nearly three o'clock, which means I'm supposed to be on my way home to meet the hair and makeup team Tucker hired for my rehearsal dinner. I sigh. I needed to leave fifteen minutes ago.

Do I think it's a bit over the top to have your hair and makeup done for a rehearsal dinner? *Of course.* But that's just how things seem to be done in Tucker's world, so I try not to complain. Besides, after all the physical labor involved in running the bakery, it's nice to have someone pamper me for a change. My phone suddenly vibrates, alerting me to a new message. I pull it out, the smooth, cool surface of the screen pressing against my fingertips as I unlock it to see who's texting me. It's Monica.

Oh, great. Just what I need right now.

> How did the conversation go last night?

I take a deep breath, wondering exactly what to say. In the midst of the break-in and subsequent cleanup last night, I had forgotten about Monica's little ultimatum. I stare at the message. I am not about to get into what *really* happened. I'm sure she would have a field day if she knew that Zach actually showed up at the shop and informed Tucker himself.

And really, it's none of her business.

I write back, my fingers dancing across the screen.

> I told him. Everything's fine.

It really pains me to send that message because, honestly, I don't think what's going on between me and Tucker is any of her business. But I swallow my pride and hit send. I'll be stuck with Monica for a long time, so I guess I have to play nice.

> I'm glad to hear that.

Then a few bubbles pop up while she writes another a message.

Looking forward to tonight.

I roll my eyes. Of course *she's* looking forward to tonight —she'll jump at any chance to hold court with her flock of friends. Part of me is looking forward to tonight too. After all, it's another step closer to marrying Tucker. But I can't shake nerves that have been building over the last couple of days. *What if something goes wrong?*

I'd be lying if I said a small part of me doesn't wish for a quiet night in with Tucker instead. Just us, some takeout, and no pressure. But regardless of how I'm feeling, the hair and makeup team is waiting for me, and soon Tucker will be too.

I put away my phone and turn the lock on my office. The back door clicks shut behind me as I head for my car, my heels clicking against the tiled floor. Just as I step outside, my phone rings, the shrill sound cutting through the air. These days, I don't receive many personal calls; most are just spam or telemarketing offers. Part of me wants to let it go to voice-mail, but curiosity gets the better of me and I pull out my phone.

When I see the name on the screen, my heart sinks.

No, it couldn't be. I steel myself, taking a deep breath before answering the phone.

"Hello?" I say, my voice sounding strained even to my own ears.

"Hello, my dear Reese. Guess what? I was able to make it down today after all. What time is the rehearsal dinner?"

The familiar voice on the other end of the line makes my stomach tingle with nerves. Things are about to get infinitely more complicated.

CHAPTER TWENTY-FOUR

My mother is here.

I nearly drop the phone right there in the parking lot, my body electric with the news. I'd be lying if I said I was happy about her arrival. She is literally the last person on earth I want to see right now, considering everything else I'm dealing with. *But she's your mother,* I tell myself. *And this is your wedding...*not to mention the fact that I did invite her. I tighten my grip on the phone.

I was just secretly hoping she wouldn't come.

Our relationship has always been complicated. My father, a successful investment banker, traveled constantly for work, leaving my stay-at-home mom and me together. However, instead of doting on me with fresh-baked cookies when I arrived home from school or spending late nights eating popcorn and watching movies with me, my mother constantly distracted herself with a toxic combination of gossip, pain pills, and alcohol.

She was an addict through and through.

By the time I was ten years old, I was cooking all of the meals and pretty much taking care of her. My father tried to be patient and take care of her, which I admired, but he was never home enough to really make a difference. So, it ended up being me taking care of my mother. When I was twelve years old, my world shattered as my father passed away from a massive heart attack. Not only was I devastated by the loss of my father, but I was also uncertain about how I was going to make it to eighteen years old and graduate high school. If my mother was hooked on pain pills and alcohol before, things only got worse after his death. She was sad and depressed, often going weeks without leaving the house.

If it wasn't for my Grandma Mae stepping in to help our family, I don't know what we would've done. Grandma Mae showed up at the house every evening, cooking us meals and, of course, teaching me how to bake. Her presence brought a sense of stability and comfort to our lives during those difficult times.

Eventually, in my senior year of high school, my mother was shipped off to rehab. Grandma Mae stayed with me, ensuring that I got all my homework done, had three square meals a day, and graduated. I was so grateful for her help and loved her dearly. She was more of a mother to me than my own mother ever could've been.

By the time my mother got out of rehab, I was already in college. She managed to blow through most of our inheritance, especially my portion of it. The only saving grace was that I was able to graduate from college without any debt, thanks to the remaining funds and scholarships I had secured.

But after that? I was on my own, left to navigate the

world without the support of my parents and relying on the strength and resilience I had developed over the years.

"Hi, Mom. How are you doing?"

"I'm doing wonderful, dear. I'm just checking into my room at the Charleston Place Hotel now. Thank you for putting me up. Of course, I still need all the details for this fabulous wedding! I can't wait to see you, honey," she gushes, her words slightly muddled.

"I can't wait to see you either, Mom," I reply, the words coming out of my mouth a complete lie. "Thanks for coming to our wedding."

"Of course, of course. I wouldn't miss it. And I look forward to seeing that lovely boy who showed me around on my last visit. Zach, was it?"

"Yes, that was Zach, but um, I'm marrying Tucker now. So..."

"Oh yes, Tucker, of course."

My cheeks burn. I have been dating Tucker for almost a year.

How could she mess that up?

After I relocated to Somerville and launched my shop, my mother stopped by for a visit. She was there to see the store and check up on me in my new life. For once, she arrived without any signs of intoxication, and I caught a glimpse of the woman I remembered from my youth. Her nails were perfectly manicured, and her hair was glossy and straight. She had that twinkle in her eye and an undeniable charm that must have captivated my father.

At the time, I was dating Zach. The two of them instantly hit it off, their laughter and easy conversation filling the air as they bonded over shared interests and experiences.

She joined Zach and me on several outings, including dinner and a visit to a few of the historical sites of Charleston. My mother *adored* Zach. She thought he was the perfect man for me and told me numerous times that I should lock him down before some Southern belle came along and swiped him right from under my nose.

So, needless to say, Zach made an impression on her.

"Listen, Mom, I'm really busy right now. I'll send you over the details for the rehearsal dinner tonight and, of course, the itinerary for the wedding this weekend. The hotel can take care of your transportation, and we can catch up later, okay?"

"That sounds fabulous, dear. I love you," she says, her voice dripping with false affection.

"You too," I muster.

I hang up the phone and tuck it into my purse, my stomach churning with a whole new level of anxiety. My mother has a way of completely embarrassing herself and me. If she shows up drunk at this wedding, I don't know what I'm going to do.

My mother's second visit coincided with the grand opening of Couture Cakes. I felt hopeful and proud, eager for her to witness my hard work come to life. However, when she arrived, the composed version of her I had previously seen was gone. Instead, she was visibly intoxicated, her breath heavy with the smell of alcohol. Zach, showing remarkable tact, gently ushered her out the door and drove her back to the hotel.

I still feel like I owe him for his help that day.

Of course, Tucker also knows about my mother's alcoholism—he was the one who suggested I invite her. But I don't think he fully grasps the potential complications her presence might bring. I'm going to need his support this evening, and I'm hoping he might know someone who can discreetly keep an eye on her. Having a designated escort could help prevent any embarrassing situations for both of us.

My phone buzzes again, and I suspect it might be my mother calling once more. I take a deep breath, steeling myself for another painful conversation, wondering how I'm going to navigate this delicate situation without letting my mother's addiction ruin the most important day of my life.

When I pick up the phone, I see that it's a message from Snaptalk, a profile I don't recognize. My heart sinks. I don't know how much more of this I can take. Part of me doesn't want to read the message because of the unsettling texts I keep receiving, but the other part of me finds it absolutely irresistible.

I open the car door and settle into the driver's seat before turning on the ignition. With a deep breath, I open my phone and read the message.

I'm going to give you one more chance to call off the wedding. Otherwise, I'll stop the wedding for you. Tick tock.

A few seconds later, the message disappears, leaving no trace.

I sit in my car and let out a loud scream, the frustration and fear threatening to overwhelm me. This is just too much. I cannot take this anymore. In a fit of anger, I throw my phone onto the floor of the car and jam the gear into reverse. I want to rip down the street, but when I see Mr. and Mrs. Hendrix from the café down the street watching me, I force myself to collect my composure. I take six deep breaths, inhaling through my mouth and exhaling through my nose, desperately trying to hold myself together.

As I navigate the winding roads back to our house, my mind is racing faster than the speedometer. The lush green trees and picturesque houses blur past my window, but I barely register them. *I have to talk to Tucker,* I think, gripping the steering wheel tighter. *He needs to know how serious this is getting.* Maybe he's found something, some clue to who would be sending these messages. I make a mental note to pull him aside as soon as we arrive at the rehearsal dinner, to find a quiet corner where we can talk.

As I turn onto our street, I feel a flicker of relief at the sight of the hairstylist's and makeup artist's cars parked out front, gleaming in the afternoon sun. *At least something's going according to plan,* I think wryly, pulling into the cool dimness of the garage.

I reach down to the floor of the car, my fingers fumbling for my phone. The screen is mercifully blank, no new messages to taunt me. I shoot a quick text to Tucker, my thumbs flying over the keys.

> Need to talk. Any updates?

I hit send, hoping that he'll have some news.

With one last deep breath, I step out of the car, the concrete cool and solid beneath my feet. *You can do this,* I tell myself, squaring my shoulders and pasting a smile on my face. *Just take it one step at a time.*

I make my way inside the house, the air conditioning hitting me like a blast of arctic air. Our housekeeper must have already let in the hair and makeup artist, because they are all set up in the living room. They rush to greet me with their bright and bubbly voices.

As they work, I force myself to respond in kind, to laugh and chatter as if everything's fine, as if my world isn't crumbling around me.

CHAPTER TWENTY-FIVE

Hours later, I'm transformed. My makeup has been expertly applied and I'm wearing an ivory dress that is so soft it feels like liquid silk. Tucker surprised me with the dress earlier this week, along with a pair of teardrop pearl earrings.

The reflection in the mirror is hardly recognizable, and for a moment, I feel like an imposter in my own skin. Scrape away all the makeup and the elaborate hairstyle, and I'm just a plain Jane girl. But I know when Tucker and I stand at the head of the table tonight, it will look like we belong together. Tucker has never given me any indication that he has any expectations about how I'm supposed to look or whom I'm supposed to be—he's always told me he loves me for whom I am. But I cannot deny the confidence instilled by the exquisite dress and impeccable styling.

I feel like I belong.

In the rush of getting ready for the rehearsal dinner, Tucker and I have barely had a moment to speak. I was hoping we'd have a few minutes to discuss the game plan to ensure my mother stays out of trouble, but all I managed to tell him was that she was here and that she might be getting a little drunk. I haven't shared a lot of details about my upbringing with Tucker, other than just what he needs to know: It wasn't great, it was *rocky*, and my mother was addicted to pain pills and alcohol. Of course, sending her to rehab over the years would help her for a while, but then she'd revert right back to her old ways.

As we go through the final preparations for the evening's rehearsal dinner, I find myself feeling disappointed and frustrated that she still hasn't arrived. Despite sending a driver to pick her up, she is nowhere in sight. I keep glancing over my shoulder, hoping to see her walking through the door, but each time I am met with disappointment. As we finish rehearsing the ceremony without her, I wonder what could be keeping her and if this is a sign of things to come.

Don't get me wrong, I want my mother to be here, to be present and sober, to share in this moment with me. But deep down, I wish she weren't here. With everything else that's going on, it feels like the whole weekend is teetering on the edge of disaster. And my drunk mother has a way of tipping things toward chaos. I take a deep breath, pushing those thoughts to the back of my mind. Tonight is about celebrating the love Tucker and I share, and I refuse to let my mother's struggles overshadow that.

The ceremony itself is quite simple. Since we don't have any bridesmaids or groomsmen, the rehearsal is straightforward. We walk down the aisle together, hold hands, look into each other's eyes as we recite our vows, and then exit. Honestly, rehearsals never made much sense to me. If you've been to a couple of weddings, you know what to expect. But I will still try to make the most of it and enjoy another delicious dinner with friends.

Well, Tucker's friends anyway.

Tonight's guest list includes around seventy-five people. For a moment, I considered just asking Tucker if we could get married here and now. All the important people in our lives are already here, so why not? It would be so much simpler than going through all the fuss tomorrow. But I quickly push that thought away. Of course I want to have the full wedding experience—walking down the aisle in a beautiful white dress and cutting into Bernie's stunning cake. It's every little girl's dream, after all.

The Magnolia Plantation grounds are a sight to behold. Ancient oak trees, their branches adorned with delicate Spanish moss, stand like gentle giants, casting intricate shadows across the lush landscape. The air is filled with the intoxicating fragrance of gardenias and magnolias, their blossoms a pristine white against the vibrant green foliage. The plantation's beauty is ethereal, as if plucked straight from a fairy tale.

Our rehearsal dinner takes place outdoors, where Elsa has orchestrated yet another flawless event. Long tables draped in crisp white tablecloths stretch out before us, adorned with organic arrangements that showcase a tasteful palette of white and pale green. It's a far cry from the hog roasts that characterize rehearsal dinners back home in Tennessee. In fact, this setting rivals the most elegant weddings I've ever attended.

As I'm about to take my seat beside Tucker, I feel a hand gently touching the back of my arm. "Reese, darling, you look absolutely beautiful," a familiar voice says. I turn around to face my mother, her presence catching me off guard amidst the picturesque surroundings.

Like me, she has the same fiery red hair, although hers is

cropped to her shoulders. It's been years since I've seen her, and she looks older, more haggard. The sight almost takes my breath away. Her eyes are dull and slightly bloodshot, but she did manage to put some makeup on and is wearing a rather pretty blue cocktail dress that shimmers in the soft evening light.

"Hello, Mother," I say, forcing a smile. "I'm so glad you're here."

We embrace, and the scent of her perfume—lavender with a hint of vanilla—transports me. Suddenly, I'm twelve again, wearing my prized blue dress at my first piano recital. The auditorium buzzes with proud parents, but Mom's seat remains empty. Later, I would learn she'd chosen a bottle of wine over my performance.

This memory floods me with conflicting emotions—the desperate need for approval, the sting of abandonment, her perpetual absence even when physically present. The familiar cocktail of love and disappointment tightens my chest. Almost involuntarily, I pull away from her embrace.

"Look at you, my dear. You are all grown up." She brushes a long strand of hair over my shoulder, her touch soft and her eyes moist. For a moment, I really see her. Her face is open and earnest. "I'm so proud of you. You look absolutely beautiful."

"Thank you, Mom." I feel my own eyes well up with tears. It's like all the words I ever wanted to hear when I was a child. Tucker suddenly appears by my side.

"You must be Mrs. Montgomery," he says, extending his hand.

She flicks a bit of red hair over her shoulder, raking her eyes up and down his frame. "What gave me away?"

"Mom, this is Tucker Harding, my fiancé."

"Well, aren't you a sight for sore eyes," she drawls, her voice dripping with charm. "Reese never mentioned how gorgeous you are."

I expect him to blush, but he doesn't miss a beat. I guess he's probably used to women gushing over him for most of his life, but it's hard not to feel a twinge of unease about the whole interaction.

"You are so kind, Mrs. Montgomery. I trust you're enjoying your stay at the Charleston Place Hotel?"

"Oh yes, it's absolutely beautiful. Thank you for putting me up."

He reaches over and gives her a slight kiss on the cheek. Now she's the one who's blushing. "I'm so glad you could make it, Mrs. Montgomery. Excuse me, I have to speak with some of our other guests."

As Tucker walks away, my mother turns to me, her eyes wide. "Oh my, Reese, he is so charming. And handsome too." She lets her eyes float around the room. "And obviously rich," she adds.

"I know, Mom, I know." Some of the connection I felt earlier is now gone. She's back to the version of herself I recognize from my childhood. "Thanks for coming," I say, trying to keep my tone light.

"Of course, dear. I wouldn't miss it for the world," she assures me, patting my arm. "Now, I know you have a lot of guests to speak with. I don't want to get in your way. I'm just going to go over to the bar and have one little drink."

My heart sinks at her words, a familiar sense of dread washing over me. "Mom, please do not get drunk," I plead, my voice barely above a whisper.

"Reese, listen, I am fine. Over the years, I've learned how

to control myself," she says, waving off my concern with a dismissive gesture.

I want to argue with her, but I decide it's better not to cause a scene. "Okay, Mom, we'll talk later," I concede, watching helplessly as she walks away, the blue fabric of her dress floating in the warm evening breeze.

She says she's going to have just one drink, but I know better. The sinking feeling in my stomach grows heavier with each step she takes toward the bar, and I can only hope that somehow, tonight will be different. But deep down, I know it won't be. *It never is.*

ABOUT AN HOUR LATER, the cocktail reception ends, and all of our guests settle into the long banquet tables for dinner. Elsa has planned an exquisite meal for us, starting with a course of smoked salmon and caviar, followed by a pear glaze salad and succulent lamb chops.

My mother has been seated about five seats down from me at the head table. I find myself glancing over at her every few minutes to see how she's doing, my nerves on edge. At one point, I catch her gesturing to the bartender to bring her another glass of wine, her movements exaggerated and slightly unsteady. The way she's slouching in her chair and the glassiness in her eyes tell me that she's probably drunk by now. *Great.*

I try to focus on the conversations around me, the laughter and chatter of our guests filling the air, but my attention keeps drifting back to my mother. It's hard not to worry about what she might do or say, the fear of her causing a scene gnawing at the pit of my stomach. I take a deep breath, trying to calm my nerves, but the tension in my body refuses to dissipate.

As the evening progresses, I watch helplessly as my mother becomes more and more intoxicated, her words slurring together and her laughter becoming louder and more inappropriate. I can feel the eyes of our guests on her, the whispers and pointed looks making my cheeks burn with embarrassment. I want to go over to her, to tell her to stop, but I know it's useless. She's too far gone, lost in the haze of alcohol that has consumed her for as long as I can remember.

On the other hand, Tucker's parents, Elaine and Charles Harding, are the epitome of Southern gentility. Elaine, with her expertly styled silver hair and string of heirloom pearls, exudes an air of refined elegance. Charles, tall and distinguished with a neatly trimmed beard, commands respect with his mere presence. They are the kind of couple that people whisper about in reverent tones, the pillars of Charleston society.

As they stand up to give their speech, I can feel the room collectively hold its breath. Elaine's voice is soft and melodic, her words painting a picture of Tucker as a young boy—curious, kind-hearted, and always eager to lend a helping hand. She regales the crowd with tales of his childhood adventures, his academic achievements, and his unwavering loyalty to family and friends. And of course, how God gave them a miracle by allowing them to adopt such a beautiful soul.

Charles takes over, his baritone voice filled with pride as he speaks of Tucker's successful career, his keen business acumen, and his dedication to carrying on the Harding legacy. While the sun sets behind him, he raises his glass, his eyes misty with emotion, and toasts to the bright future that lies ahead for his son and his new bride.

As the entire crowd erupts in applause, I glance at Tucker, catching a mix of joy and slight embarrassment on his face. He's beaming, clearly touched by his father's words, even as he ducks his head modestly. I feel a small pang of envy. What must it be like, to have parents who support you unconditionally, who celebrate your every triumph and cushion your every fall?

My gaze drifts to my own mother, seated at a table in the corner. She's already on her third glass of wine, her cheeks flushed and her eyes glazed. I can practically see the wheels turning in her head.

So I sit there, my smile frozen on my face, my nerves stretched taut as a wire. And I pray that somehow, someway, we'll make it through this night unscathed. Then my mother stands up with her glass in hand and says six words that nearly cause me to pass out.

"I'd like to make a toast."

CHAPTER TWENTY-SIX

Without thinking, my hand travels up my beautiful designer dress to rest on my heart. It's beating so fast I almost feel like I need to hold it in place. Beads of sweat are forming on my forehead and under my arms, the cool evening breeze doing little to alleviate the heat that seems to radiate from my body.

An evening that felt like it was flying by suddenly slows down to a crawl. I watch my mother holding the lipstick-stained wine glass in her hand, her fingers wrapped around the stem in a white-knuckled grip. It wobbles slightly, the Chardonnay swishing from side to side as she gets up to her feet, her movements unsteady.

I can feel Tucker's hand on my knee, trying to comfort me. He doesn't know a lot about my mother, but anyone can see that she's drunk, her eyes glazed over and her speech slurred. I brace myself for what my mother is about to say, my heart pounding in my chest as she opens her mouth.

"Hello. My name is Georgia Montgomery. Most of you here don't know me, but I am Reese's mother," she begins, her voice too loud in the suddenly quiet setting. "Reese has always been a special child. From the time she was small, she was determined. Determined to make good grades in class, determined to take care of me, and of course, determined to become a successful pastry chef..." She trails off, her words slurring together as she sways on her feet.

I look around me. No one seems to notice she's drunk, and even if they do they keep their facial expressions neutral. *Okay, so far, so good. This isn't too bad.*

"As many of you know or may not know, her father passed away a few years ago. It's been very difficult for me, but Reese is always thinking of me. Always sending a card or flowers or calling me on the phone," she continues, her voice thick with emotion.

Now we're getting into uncharted territory. I'm not sure if the wine has gone to her head, but she seems to be making things up at this point—or she's trying to drop me some serious hints about my lack of communication lately. I have not sent cards or flowers, not since...I can't even remember.

If I'm being honest with myself, the bakery has been a convenient shield. Eighteen-hour days kneading dough and decorating cakes left little time for family drama. But that's just an excuse, isn't it? The real reason I've been absent is far more complex. Every missed call, every unanswered text message was a small act of self-preservation. It's easier to lose myself in the warm aroma of fresh bread than to navigate the minefield of our relationship.

I take a moment to glance around the table and see that all the guests have given her their full attention, their eyes wide and their mouths slightly agape. They're literally hanging on her every word. I feel my hands grip the front of my white dress, the fabric bunching beneath my fingers.

"And of course, I've always wanted the best for Reese.

So, tonight, when I saw her standing next to her fiancé, I was overjoyed. He and I met a few years ago, and he was so kind and caring toward me. I know that he'll do everything he can to take the best care of Reese," she says, her words coming out in a rush.

Met a few years ago? I dare to look at Tucker, who seems oblivious to her mistake. I only met Tucker a year ago, unless she's thinking...*oh no*.

"So, will everyone raise their glass and help me in celebrating the marriage of Reese Montgomery and Zach Caldwell."

Oh no, no, no.

She did *not*.

My mother, in her drunken state, has forgotten whom I am marrying. I suddenly feel like I'm suffocating, my lungs constricting as I struggle to breathe, the air around me suddenly unbreathable. There is a deafening silence around the room as everyone holds their breath, their eyes wide and their expressions a mix of shock and sympathy. Tucker is bright red, his face as flushed as my own, the embarrassment and anger radiating off him in waves.

What should I do?

I can feel the eyes of our guests on us, their gazes heavy. I steal a glimpse at Monica, who is sitting upright in her seat, her glass hanging in the air and a Cheshire grin on her face. I want nothing more than to sink into the ground and disappear. But I know I can't do that. Especially after what happened last night between Tucker, Zach, and me. *Think, Reese, think!*

I know I must confront this situation before it unravels further. Taking a deep breath to calm my racing thoughts, I stand, pushing my chair back as gracefully as possible. My hand trembles as I raise my glass, causing the champagne bubbles to dance erratically. Despite the tightness in my chest, I search for the right words to salvage the moment.

"Thank you, Mother, for that heartfelt speech. Your presence here tonight means the world to me, and I'm so grateful that you made the effort to be with us, despite the challenges you sometimes face with your memory." I pause for a moment, allowing the words to resonate with the audience, a subtle acknowledgment of my mother's slipup.

My mother scrunches up her face slightly, and for a moment I think she might argue with me. I can see the thought written across her face: *What memory troubles?* Regardless, I continue, keeping my eyes trained on her and willing her to be silent.

"I know that your love for Tucker and me is unwavering, and that you only want the very best for us as we embark on this new chapter in our lives." I turn to face the room, making eye contact with the guests, a warm smile on my lips. The energy of the room has shifted and I can see a wave of understanding rippling across each face at the table. Even Caroline Louise looks a little misty eyed. That's when I know it's working.

I take a deep breath, bolstering the emotion in my voice as I continue. "I know that many of you have experienced the bittersweet joy of having family members who have passed on, or who may be facing their own struggles, be it with memory or other challenges that life can bring." I give a small, understanding nod toward my mother. She continues to look perplexed.

"In moments like these, we are reminded of the precious-ness of the time we have with our loved ones, and the importance of cherishing every moment, every memory, every laugh and every tear."

I reach out and take Tucker's hand, squeezing it gently as I speak. To his credit, he squeezes back, and I realize he's buying into this as much as everyone else. *Thank goodness.*

"As Tucker and I stand on the brink of our new life together, we are so incredibly blessed to know that we have your unwavering support, your love, and your guidance to help us navigate whatever twists and turns the future may bring. So thank you, from the bottom of our hearts. We are so grateful for each and every one of you."

As I finish my speech, I can see the emotion on the faces of the guests, the nods of understanding and the teary eyes of those who have been touched by my words. Tucker stands, pulling me in close and placing a light kiss on my forehead.

It looks like I've managed to avoid a catastrophe, *for now.*

CHAPTER TWENTY-SEVEN

A few moments later, Tucker drops my hand and reaches for the fork at his place setting. He smooths his tuxedo jacket and adjusts his bow tie. The sun has nearly set, casting a warm, golden glow across the outdoor space. Spanish moss sways gently from ancient oak branches overhead, mimicking the sway of the conversations below. Tucker takes a deep breath, his eyes meeting mine briefly before he gently taps his champagne glass.

"Can I have your attention, please?" The murmurs around the table settle back into silence. I steal a quick look at my mother, who remains silent, her eyes focused on the glass in front of her. Everyone else is now looking to Tucker.

"I just want to say how blessed I am to have everyone here tonight, celebrating with us." His voice is strong and steady as he speaks. "I think Reese has already done a beautiful job of communicating how we feel, so I can only echo her words by saying thank you. Each of you mean so much to me, and I'm grateful you're here to celebrate this important moment in my life."

He shifts his weight, and raises his glass a bit higher. "But most of all, I'm blessed to have such an amazing fiancée by my side. Reese, you are the love of my life, and I can't wait to start our forever together. Cheers."

He turns to me, his eyes shining, and I feel my heart swell. He leans in to kiss me at the cheers of the crowd. In this moment, I'm overwhelmed by gratitude for Tucker's unwavering support. He's stood by me through Mom's social blunders, forgiven my lie about working with Zach, and cleaned up my shop after the break-in, even though I'm sure he was angry.

Every time I think he's going to turn on me for a mistake I've made, he proves otherwise. Despite the rocky path we've navigated, Tucker's love remains constant. And maybe that's what I've always loved about him. He's a true ally—someone who sees beyond my flaws and loves me unconditionally.

After we all sit down and the toast is complete, the dessert portion of the dinner continues, the sweet aroma of chocolate and vanilla wafting through the air. Tucker begins chatting with his dad, who is on the other side of us in the seating arrangement. I look down the table and notice my mother getting up to use the restroom.

I seize the opportunity to speak with her. I get up from my seat, murmuring a word to Tucker before following her to the bathroom. I don't see her at first. She must be in one of the stalls, so I wait silently until she's finished, my heart pounding in my chest.

Yes, I managed to deflect her mistake about Zach, convincing everyone she's suffering from mental lapses. But a nagging doubt lingers. Did she really mix up names, or was this a calculated move? A part of me can't shake the feeling that this was deliberate—her way of punishing me for my prolonged absence.

She steps out of the stall and the two of us make eye contact.

"Oh hello, dear," she says, her glassy eyes fixing on mine. "What a lovely dinner this has been. Thank you again for including me." Her words come out contorted and slurred. She stumbles almost imperceptibly as she brushes past me to wash her hands. I watch her hand shake as she reaches for a towel.

If she wasn't fully drunk during her speech, she certainly is now.

"Mother," I say, my voice tight with frustration. "How could you?"

She freezes, her hands dripping with water, and looks at me. "What do you mean? I said congratulations to you and Tucker, didn't I?"

"No, Mom, you congratulated me and Zach. Don't you remember?"

Her face is blank. "No," she says, nodding softly.

The open look of innocence and confusion on her face stops me in my tracks. I bite my lip. Even though my speech about her memory issues was fabricated, it might actually be true. My mother really does seem confused, her eyes clouded with uncertainty. I feel a small pang of guilt. Maybe it was an honest mistake after all.

"Oh no, did I mess up your dinner?" she says. "Reese, I'm so sorry."

I tip my head to the side, studying her. She seems suddenly small, almost helpless. I've read that alcoholism can bring on early onset dementia. I guess I've been so busy I never thought to check on her.

"Don't worry about it," I say softly, my anger dissipating slightly. "Just keep in mind in the future his name is Tucker, okay?"

"Okay," she says quietly, almost as if a child has been scolded, her shoulders slumping slightly. "I'm sorry, Reese. I didn't mean to cause any trouble."

I sigh, taking in her slightly disheveled appearance and the way she sways on her feet. "You look like you've had a little too much to drink. Would you like to have someone take you back to the hotel?"

My mother, who is ever proud and never wants to admit defeat, gives a small nod, her eyes downcast. "Actually, I am feeling rather tired. Yes, that would be lovely. Can you call me a driver?"

"Of course." I wrap my arms around my mother and escort her to the front of the gallery, the cool night air a welcome relief from the stuffiness inside. Although it's the last thing I want to think about right now, getting care for my mother might be my next priority after this wedding is over.

I signal one of the drivers that Tucker has assembled for the party and give them the address of the hotel. I tuck my mother into the backseat of the sleek black car, turn on my heel, and prepare to return to the rehearsal dinner, my heart feeling lighter with each step.

I now have one less thing to worry about. For now, anyway.

As I round the corner of the building, the sound of hushed whispers stops me in my tracks. I instantly recognize Tucker's voice, low and urgent, but the other voice is unfamiliar—a man with a heavy accent.

I know I shouldn't eavesdrop, but something about the tension in their voices, the furtive glances they cast around the deserted hallway, roots me to the spot. I press myself against the wall, straining to catch their words over the distant clatter of dishes and the murmur of conversation from the reception.

"Listen, Tucker," the man hisses, his voice thick with a Russian accent. "We had a deal. You promised me the shipment would be here by now, no questions asked."

Tucker's reply is muffled, but I can hear an edge in his voice. "I know, Sergei. But there were complications. The customs agents were sniffing around, asking too many questions. I had to lie low for a while, let things cool off."

Sergei scoffs, his voice dripping with disdain. "Excuses. That's all I ever hear from you, Tucker. Excuses and empty promises. Do you have any idea how much money I'm losing every day those goods sit in some warehouse, gathering dust?"

There's a pause, a heavy silence that seems to stretch on for an eternity. When Tucker speaks again, his voice is quiet but firm. "I'll make it right, Sergei. I always do. Just give me a little more time."

"Time?" he spits, his voice rising in anger. "I've given you nothing but time, Tucker. And what do I have to show for it? A bunch of cheap knockoffs that I can't move, and a sea of angry customers breathing down my neck."

Cheap knockoffs? What is he talking about?

But before I can even begin to process their conversation, Sergei is speaking again. "You have one week, Tucker. One week to get me those goods, or else."

"Or else what?"

Sergei laughs, a harsh, mirthless sound that jangles my nerves. "Or else I'll have to take matters into my own hands. And trust me, you don't want to know what that means."

I hear the sound of footsteps receding down the hall, the slam of a door that seems to echo like a gunshot in the stillness. I stand there for a long moment, my heart pounding in my chest, my mind spinning with a thousand questions.

What has Tucker gotten himself into?

CHAPTER TWENTY-EIGHT

I slip around the corner and Tucker slides into view. He's standing perfectly still, staring after Sergei. I close the distance between us, coming up beside him and taking his hand.

"Tucker, is everything okay?" I ask.

He turns back to me and I see a look flash across his eyes. He wipes a bit of sweat from his brow and tugs at the collar of his jacket.

"I've been looking for you everywhere," he says. "Yes, everything's fine."

Really? Because it sounded to me like he just received an open threat from one of his business associates. I open my mouth to argue, but decide against it. We can discuss work after the wedding, I suppose. I'm not looking to ruffle any feathers right now, especially after my mother's speech.

"Let's head back to the party. My parents would like to grab a couple of photos," he says, brushing a lock of hair over my shoulder. He grabs my hand and starts to take a few steps in the direction of the reception outside. I stop, pulling him back to face me.

"Tucker..." I swallow the lump in my throat. "I'm really sorry about my mom. I didn't know she was going to say—"

He shakes his head. "It's okay, I understand. She obviously has some problems and she must've met Zach when she came into town during your bakery opening, right?" I confirm with a slight nod. "I'm not upset. Honestly, you handled it beautifully. You took what was an awkward moment and turned it into something wonderful." He leans in and kisses me deeply. "Just another reason I love you more."

I can't even begin to describe the buzz from my lips to my toes as he kisses me.

"I'm so glad you understand," I say as he gently pulls away. *So glad,* I think. But the conversation I just witnessed between him and Sergei still gnaws at me. I want to know what's going on, but I'm afraid to ask.

"You know if there's anything going on that you need to talk about, you can always talk to me about it, right?"

"Of course, always," he says. "Now, our guests are waiting for us."

I let him take my hand, letting the topic drop for now. He guides me back outside to the dinner area, where the string lights are now twinkling in the sunset. We walk over to the bar where his parents are waiting. They each compliment me on what a lovely speech I gave, and we take a couple of photos together.

"Reese," I hear the shrill voice of Monica coming up on my right. I turn to face her, my body tensing up at her presence. She's impeccably dressed in a sleek black designer cocktail dress and nude heels. She's also wearing a smile that doesn't quite reach her eyes. "Hello, darling. It's so good to see you. You look absolutely stunning in this dress."

"Hello, Monica," I say, forcing a smile onto my face. "Thank you."

Tucker lets go of my hand, stepping toward a group of guests who have flagged him down to get his attention. *Don't leave me alone with her,* I plead silently, but he's already gone, swallowed up by the crowd. Monica and I are now left facing each other, a ball of tension hanging in the air between us.

"So, that was quite a speech your mother gave," she says, dusting an invisible speck of lint from her dress as she delicately sips her cocktail. "I do hope she gets better."

I bet you do, I think, my jaw clenching.

"Yes, she's been having some problems with her memory," I say, reiterating the point I'd already made in my speech. I can only imagine the side conversations Monica has been having since my mother's gaffe about Zach. It will be the gossip of the week, I'm sure.

"Her memory, *right*," she says, a thinly veiled look of doubt on her face. Even though I want to smack the expression right off her face, there is something more pressing on my mind.

"Monica, can I ask you something?" I lean in, trying to keep my voice casual.

"Of course, Reese, anything," she replies, her tone overly sweet. Her smile doesn't quite reach her eyes.

"What happened between Charlotte and Tucker? Why did she leave him?"

Monica blinks rapidly, a faint blush creeping up her neck. "Oh...well, to be honest, I don't really know. There are some vapid rumors about where she wandered off to, but no one knows the truth."

"But you knew them better than anyone," I press. "Did you notice they were having problems? Did Tucker ever tell you what happened?"

Monica twirls her glass, her manicured nails tapping against the stem. She studies me for a moment, her eyes narrowing slightly. "Charlotte wasn't the strongest person. She always struggled with stress, even in high school." She leans in, lowering her voice. "Some might even say she was unstable. I didn't love them together, but Tucker was ready to settle down, so..." She trails off, taking a long sip of champagne. "Anyway, it doesn't surprise me that she snapped under the pressure and ran off. Why do you ask?"

"It's just that I've been getting some strange messages. Saying that I should call off the wedding. And I thought maybe...Charlotte was back and trying to ruin the wedding."

Monica furrows her brow, studying me. She opens her mouth to say something, then closes it. It's the first time I've even seen her off-balance. She begins again. "I don't know who would be sending those, but I know it's not Charlotte. She is the one who left him, remember?"

That's exactly what Zach said. I open my mouth to probe further, but Monica's attention suddenly shifts. Her eyes dart to the opposite side of the bar.

"Oops. Listen, dear, I have to go. My husband's flagging me down. Looks like he's in a deep conversation with Caroline Louise and is in need of a rescue." Before I can respond, Monica flips her glossy locks over her shoulder and sashays away, her hips swaying as she weaves through the crowd.

I watch her go, a mix of emotions swirling inside me. Part of me can't stand Monica—her fake charm, her obvious disdain barely hidden beneath a veneer of politeness. But I also feel a small flicker of gratitude. For all her faults, she's the first person to share anything concrete about Charlotte and Tucker's relationship. It's not much, but it's a start.

As I mull over the words she used...*troubled, unstable, snapped...* I realize I'm no closer to understanding what really happened. But at least now I have a piece of the puzzle. Clearly Charlotte wasn't as put together as she made everyone believe.

The question is, do I really want to see the whole picture?

Before I can dwell on the situation further, I suddenly realize that in the hustle to follow my mother, I have left my purse on the dinner table. I walk back over to retrieve it and see that it's still hanging from the back of the chair. Out of habit, I unlock my phone and check it when I open the lid. I should be mingling with the other guests right now, but instead, I'm worried about my mother and want to make sure she arrived safely at her hotel room.

I can see I have several Snaptalk messages, one from Zach checking in and then one from an unknown profile. I bite my lip. *Do I want to read the message? Do I even want to know what ridiculous accusation is waiting for me?*

When I open the message, I realize it's not a text but a photo. A bit of bile crawls up my throat. I need to talk to Tucker, *now.*

CHAPTER TWENTY-NINE

I stand perfectly still at the head of the decorated table, holding the phone in my trembling hand. It's hard to describe in words what I'm seeing, but I look at the photo and read the message again, my heart pounding in my chest.

The photograph itself has been altered by some amateur, but the effect is still chilling. It's an engagement photo of Tucker and me, one that we shared on our social media and used to send out announcements. In the original, I am wearing a blue maxi dress, my hair blowing back over my shoulders as I gaze lovingly into Tucker's eyes. He's looking down at me, his expression filled with adoration, as we stand in front of the plantation with the Spanish moss floating in the wind behind us.

But in this twisted version, a knife has been Photoshopped into my neck, and blood is dripping all over my shoulder and down the sides of my body. Even though I can tell the photo has been altered, it still leaves a sick feeling in my stomach.

Underneath the grotesque image is a message that reads:

Time's up.

Before I have time to even process the message, I take a screenshot. Finally I will have something I can show Tucker. He needs to see this. He needs to understand it's not just harassment anymore—this is a direct threat.

But why? My mind reels with possibilities. *Who hates me enough to go to such lengths?* The two glasses of champagne I had earlier are suddenly making me feel dizzy, the room spinning around me in a blur of colors and shapes. I scan the space, looking toward the bar where Tucker was earlier, but I don't see him. Panic rises in my throat, along with a sense of helplessness that threatens to consume me.

My breath starts coming in short, shallow gasps. I can't breathe. I can't think. I need to get out of here, need to find Tucker and tell him what's happening. Before I can make a move, I see a group of socialites walking toward me, led by the unmistakable figure of Caroline. She's hard to miss in her bright yellow gown, her blonde hair cascading down her back in loose waves. Her eyes are fixed on me, a look of concern etched onto her flawless face.

There's no way I can put on airs and speak to her right now, I think, my stomach twisting in knots. I can't pretend that everything's fine, can't smile and nod and make small talk when my world is falling apart. Caroline Louise is just a few feet away now, her voice ringing out above the din of the party.

"Reese? Are you okay? You don't look—"

"I'm sorry. I need to find Tucker," I blurt out, cutting her off mid-sentence. I clutch my phone tightly in my hand, the altered photo still glowing on the screen, and rush off in the direction of the plantation building, my heart pounding in my ears.

All around me, people are mingling and laughing, their faces bright with happiness and excitement. They have no idea what's going on, no clue about the dark threats and twisted messages that have been haunting me for days.

"Reese," a familiar voice says.

I turn around to see Tucker. His face immediately turns from one of excitement to concern. He rushes up to me, placing his hands on each of my shoulders. "What's wrong?"

"We need to talk," I say, my voice quivering slightly. I look around, seeing all the people around us. "Somewhere private."

He grabs my hand and leads me into the building. My pulse slows a few beats as I feel the warmth of his skin, but the nausea remains. We stop just inside the main house, where there is a small sitting room. The room is dimly lit, with only the soft glow of a table lamp casting long shadows on the walls.

"What's going on?" he asks, his strong hands cupping my shoulders once again. I realize I'm trembling.

"Remember all those messages I told you about, and what happened at the shop?" My voice quivers as I speak, barely above a whisper.

"Yes," he replies, his eyes searching mine.

"I got another message, and whoever it is, they want me to call off the wedding."

"Let me see it," he says, his tone serious.

I show him the message, the screen illuminating his face in an eerie blue light. A dark shadow covers his features, and he bites his lip, his jaw clenching. "Who would do this?"

"I don't know. Did you find anything out from your tech guy?" I ask, hoping for some sort of lead.

He shakes his head, frustration evident in his movements. "I sent them the profile names you gave me, but without giving them your phone, they couldn't find anything."

"Tucker, do you have any idea why someone would be threatening me, why they don't want us to get married?" My voice cracks, the weight of the situation bearing down on me.

He shakes his head earnestly, his eyes wide with sincerity. "I have no idea."

"Do you think it's—" Before I can get the name out, he cuts me off, his hand gently squeezing my shoulder.

"No, I don't think it's her. Honestly, I don't know who it is."

At that point, he wraps his arms around me, pulling me in for a hug. I lean into the warmth of his embrace, feeling the strength of his muscular arms around me. The sound of his steady heartbeat against my ear makes me relax slightly, the tension in my body easing. After a few minutes, he pulls away, his hands still resting on my arms.

"Do you think we should call the police?" I ask. He glances at the phone again, considering this option.

"The police are already aware of what happened at the shop. Honestly, I don't think there's much they can do." He sighs, running a hand through his hair. "Listen, I don't think this is anything to worry about. I'm going to be with you from now until the wedding, and I won't let anything happen to you. Everything's going to be fine, okay?"

His words are reassuring, but the uneasy feeling in the pit of my stomach remains.

"Okay."

I trust Tucker. I know that he's capable and will do anything to take care of me, but there's still a nagging feeling that something else is going on, like a persistent itch I can't quite scratch. My mind races with possibilities, each one more unsettling than the last.

"Do you think you can go back into the party, or are you ready to go home?" Tucker asks, his voice soft.

A queasy sensation roils through my abdomen. There's no doubt I am upset. The thought of facing the crowd, their curious stares and whispered speculations, makes my skin crawl. "I don't think I can do it," I say, my voice barely above a whisper.

"Okay, listen. We're going to go in and say goodbye to our guests, make an excuse that we need an early night for the big day tomorrow, and then we'll go home together, okay?" His plan sounds reassuring, and I find myself nodding in agreement.

"Isn't it bad luck to spend the last night before the wedding together?" I ask, a small smile tugging at the corners of my mouth despite the situation.

Tucker shakes his head, his fingers gently brushing against my cheek, his touch warm and comforting. "We don't need luck—we have each other. We love each other. Everything's going to be okay." His words wrap around me like a warm blanket, and for a moment, I allow myself to believe him.

He leads me back into the party, the sound of laughter and clinking glasses flooding my ears. The room feels too bright, too loud, and I find myself clinging to Tucker's arm as he makes an announcement about our departure. His voice is confident and smooth, betraying none of the concern he must be feeling. Then, with his arm securely around my waist, he walks me to the car and we head home, the cool night air a welcome relief from the stuffy atmosphere of the party.

When we arrive home that evening, the familiar scent of our shared space envelops me, a mixture of Tucker's cologne and the faint aroma of the scented candles I love. I snuggle into his arms in our bed, my head resting against his chest, listening to the steady rhythm of his heartbeat. I try to focus on the positive aspects of our upcoming wedding and our future together, pushing the nagging doubts and fears to the back of my mind.

As sleep begins to claim me, the last thing I remember is the comforting weight of Tucker's arms around me, holding me close and making me feel safe, even if only for tonight.

CHAPTER THIRTY

I wake up to the sound of my phone buzzing incessantly on the nightstand, the shrill chime of my alarm piercing through the fog of my restless sleep. I reach over and silence my phone. For a moment, I lie there, staring up at the ceiling, my heart pounding. Usually I give myself a few minutes to run through my to-dos for the day at the bakery.

Then I remember. *Today is the day.* My heart flutters with nerves. *My wedding day.* Instinctively I turn over toward Tucker's side of the bed. It's empty. However, in his place is a large bouquet of white- and blush-colored roses. Even though we opted not to have a wedding party, Tucker has met a group of his college buddies at a local hotel for a groom's breakfast.

I prop myself up on my elbow and reach out to pull out the card that's been tucked in between the petals. It reads:

TO MY BEAUTIFUL BRIDE, I CAN'T WAIT TO MARRY YOU TODAY.

WITH ALL MY LOVE, TUCKER

I run my hands over the thick linen cardstock. At the top is a monogram of the letter H, and underneath are gold embossed letters with our names, Tucker & Reese Harding. The tips of my fingers hover over my new name. *Reese Harding.* I bite my lip. Changing my last name is going to take some getting used to. It was so sweet of Tucker to have stationery made for us, and for a moment I revel in his thoughtfulness.

But when I sit up, it all comes back to me. My head feels heavy, my limbs thick with exhaustion. Even though I fell soundly asleep in Tucker's arms, I woke up at three a.m., with no hope of falling asleep again. In fact, I barely slept a wink, my mind racing with worst-case scenarios and nagging doubts.

What if something goes wrong? What if my stalker shows up at the wedding with a knife? What if Tucker changes his mind? What if...

I shake my head, trying to silence the anxious voices in my mind. I have to push through the day, no matter what. Literally hundreds of eyes are going to be on me today, and I can't let Tucker down, even though I have my doubts about my own safety. A week ago my only worries were getting the gala confections right and whether or not Bernie could create the wedding cake I had envisioned. That feels like a lifetime ago. Now, I'm more concerned someone might show up at the wedding and plunge a knife in my neck.

Not a great thought to kick off your wedding day.

I push myself out of bed and head to the bathroom. A look in the mirror at my puffy cheeks and the dark circles under my eyes tells me I need to get a few under-eye patches on my face asap. There's no way I'm showing up to my wedding looking like the walking dead.

The gentle sound of chatter from downstairs reaches my ears. The hair and makeup team have let themselves in and are waiting for me. I take a quick shower and then slip into a white silk robe, the word *Bride* in delicate script across the back. When I arrive downstairs, there are half a dozen women who make up what I have chosen to refer to as my "glam squad" waiting for me. Their faces are bright with enthusiasm. They chatter excitedly as they set up their equipment, the air thick with the scent of hairspray and perfume.

I try to match their energy, but all I can feel is anxiety. I'm afraid one of them might ask me what's wrong, and the entire story will come tumbling out. To their credit, they work around me without saying a word.

Elsa, the wedding planner, suddenly appears by my side, the scent of her designer perfume wafting over me as she thrusts a steaming cappuccino into my hand. "Reese, darling, are you ready for the big day?" she says, her voice dripping with forced enthusiasm as she leads me by the elbow to a soft leather salon chair.

I settle in, the supple leather cradling my body. Around me, the makeshift salon is a flurry of activity, the air thick with the acrid scent of hairspray and the hum of blow dryers. I close my eyes, trying to let the chaos fade away, to lose myself in the moment.

But even as the stylist's fingers work through my hair, twisting and pinning and spraying, the image keeps returning to me. The altered photo of Tucker and me, the knife Photoshopped into my neck, the blood dripping down my body like a macabre waterfall. It's playing as if on a loop in my mind.

Pause, rewind, replay. *Neck, knife, blood.*

Elsa's voice cuts through my thoughts, her words a rapid-fire barrage of instructions and reminders. "Now, remember, the ceremony starts at four p.m. sharp, so we'll need to have you in the bridal suite by two thirty for final touch-ups and photos. The cocktail hour will begin immediately after the ceremony, and then we'll move into the reception at six p.m. I've arranged for a private room for you to change into your second dress before the first dance, and..."

Her words blur together, a meaningless jumble of times and locations and details that I can't seem to focus on. All I can think about is the message that accompanied the photo, the ominous threat that has been echoing in my mind since the moment I saw it.

Time's up.

Replaying the words makes my spine tingle, and a sickening sense of dread settles in. *Who hates me enough to go to such lengths to threaten me?*

"Reese? Are you alright?" Elsa's voice jolts me back to the present, her pale hand resting on my shoulder with a touch that's meant to be comforting but feels more like a vise grip.

I force a smile onto my face, hoping that the layers of makeup will hide the fear and anxiety that I know must be written all over my features.

No, I'm not. I'm not all right...

"Of course, Elsa. Just a little pre-wedding jitters, that's all." My voice sounds brittle.

She nods, her eyes narrowing slightly as she studies me for a moment. I can tell she doesn't quite believe me, that she can sense the tension radiating off me in waves. But to her credit, she doesn't push, doesn't pry into the dark thoughts that are swirling in my mind.

"Well, just remember to take deep breaths and focus on the love you and Tucker share," she says, her voice softening with a hint of genuine affection. "That's what will get you through this day, and all the days to come."

I nod, swallowing hard against the lump that rises in my throat. *If only it were that simple.* The stylist puts the finishing touches on my hair, the curls cascading down my back like a waterfall of silk. I catch a glimpse of myself in the mirror. My face has been transformed into a flawless mask of bridal perfection. The dark circles that clung to my eyes a few hours ago have been banished.

I definitely look the part.

I push the thought aside, taking one last look at myself before heading out to the waiting limo. The driver holds the door open for me, his face impassive as I slide into the plush leather seat. Tucker's probably already on his way in the white Rolls Royce, I think, picturing him looking dashing in his tuxedo.

As if on cue, I get a text message from him:

> See you at the altar. I love you.

I text, and then hit send.

> See you soon. Love you too.

I tuck the phone into the seat next to me, flipping it upside down. The limo ambles down the driveway, and I turn my attention to the lush green bushes that line our home. *Our home.* I take a deep breath. *You can do this.*

Just as the limo pulls away from the curb, my phone buzzes loudly, the sound cutting through the silence like a knife. I glance down at the screen, my heart dropping when I see a slew of text messages waiting for me from an unknown number. I hold my finger over the phone, debating whether I should delete the messages or read them.

Who would be messaging me now?

When I see the messages, my heart sinks in my chest.

> Reese! This is Bernie. My phone doesn't have reception at the Gala. So I'm messaging you from one of the waiters' phones.

> A few people here got a message on social media about a fire at the shop. They showed me pictures!

> I called the fire department and I am on my way now!

With trembling hands, I put my phone down, the heaviness of the situation threatening to crush me. *My shop...is on fire.*

My mind races through a minefield of conflicting emotions. On one side, there's the wedding—my future with Tucker, the promise of a life we've carefully planned together, with friends and family gathered to celebrate. I can almost hear the wedding march, see Tucker's face as he waits for me at the altar.

But on the other side, there's my shop—my dream realized, built from the ground up with sweat and tears. It's more than just a business; it's a piece of my soul. The thought of it burning, of losing everything I've worked so hard for, sends a physical pain through my chest.

What if the fire department can't get there in time? I could help them, show them where the ovens are, how to shut off the gas valve. In my mind's eye, I see flames licking at the cherished photo of Grandma Mae as it hangs on the wall. And her antique rolling pin, the one she used to teach me how to bake—it's irreplaceable.

Surely Tucker will understand if I'm a little late, right?

I lean forward, tapping on the partition separating me from the driver. "Change of plans," I whisper, my voice barely audible over the pounding of my heart. "I need you to take me to the bakery on Main Street. Now."

The driver's eyes meet mine in the rearview mirror, hesitation etched on his face. "But Miss Montgomery...the wedding..."

"Please," I plead, desperation clawing at my throat, tears welling in my eyes. "I don't have time to argue. Just drive me to 242 Main Street."

He nods solemnly. As the limo speeds down the road, I sink back into my seat, my mind a battlefield of emotions. The problem-solving side of my brain struggles to take control, assessing the potential damage, reassuring me that I have insurance, that I can rebuild. But the emotional side, the part of me that poured my heart and soul into this shop, threatens to consume me.

I think of my wedding cake and the gala pastries that have already been delivered, which means the worst possible scenario has been avoided. But it's not enough to stem the tide of grief that washes over me. I close my eyes, hot tears streaming down my face, ruining the perfect makeup that took hours to craft.

I attempt to call Tucker, but his phone goes to voicemail. I try my mother, but after two rings I change my mind and hang up. I'm sure she's had at least a half dozen mimosas by now. I try Tucker one more time, but it's no use. I'm sure he's turned off his phone, focusing on the wedding ahead, completely unaware that I won't be there. A pang of guilt pierces my heart, knowing that Tucker will arrive at the altar, his eyes searching for me, only to find an empty space where I should be standing. I promise myself that as soon as I meet with the fire department I will rush back to the wedding.

I just hope I make it in time.

CHAPTER THIRTY-ONE

The limo screeches to a halt in front of the bakery, the sudden stop jolting me out of my panicked thoughts. I don't wait for the driver to open the door, instead scrambling out of the car, my heart pounding, my phone clutched to my chest. The long satin folds of my dress catch in the doorway, but I manage to reach down and pull the long hem out, letting it fall on the dusty street beneath me.

The driver, dressed in a black suit, makes his way around the car toward me.

"Miss Montgomery?"

I part my lips to say something, but I can't find the words. My eyes are locked on the shop. *Something's not right.* There's no smoke, no flames, no sirens wailing in the distance. Just an eerie, unsettling silence. I stand there on the sidewalk, my white dress billowing in the breeze. *What's going on?* I wonder, my stomach twisting in knots. *Where's the fire?*

I flip over my phone and call Bernie's cell phone. It goes straight to voicemail.

I take a few steps in the direction of the front door. I need to make sure everything's okay. Bernie wouldn't have sent those messages unless there was something wrong. Maybe the smoke is coming from the back. If so, I'll call the fire department myself.

"Miss Montgomery, would you like me to wait?" The driver is staring at me as I walk away from him, a curious expression on his face.

"No," I say, finding my voice. "I just need some time to make sure everything is okay. I've got my phone and I will call you if I need anything." I hold up my phone, proving my point. "Please go to Magnolia, find Tucker and tell him I'm here. Tell him there's been an accident at the shop. Then come back for me. Can you do that?"

"Yes, ma'am."

He nods, turning his back to me as he strides back to the long black limousine. I take a step toward the shop, my white satin heels clicking on the pavement. I notice the door is slightly cracked open. *Why would Bernie leave the door open?* Maybe she was in a hurry when she left for the gala.

I step forward and gently push open the door, which still has plywood nailed on the front. I step inside, the skirt of my gown dragging across the floor, leaving a trail of delicate lace and satin in my wake.

The bakery is clean, the glass dome gleaming by the front register, just as I left it yesterday. I take a few steps inside, looking for any signs of smoke.

"Bernie? Are you there?"

I watch the dark hallway behind the counter, waiting for her to come bounding forward any minute. I'm only met with an eerie silence. "Bernie?"

I make my way around the counter, my dress dragging

behind me as it snags on one of our bistro chairs. When I reach the hallway, I smell it. *Gasoline*. The acrid, pungent odor fills my nostrils, making my eyes water and my throat burn.

Oh god, I think, my heart hammering against my ribs. *Why does my shop smell like gasoline?* I should call the fire department. My thoughts turn again to Bernie. She said she would be here. What if something happened to her? I should check in the back first. I pick up my pace, pulling up the train of my dress in my free hand as I plunge forward.

"Bernie! Can you hear me?!"

Again, I'm met with silence. I walk around the kitchen, open the walk-in refrigerator, peek into the bathroom. But there is no one here, just me. I try Bernie's cell phone one more time. It goes to voicemail. I hang up without leaving a message.

And then—a rustling sound from the back of the shop, like someone moving around in the shadows. I take a step forward, then another, my breath coming in short, sharp gasps.

"Hello?"

Something feels wrong. But I can't stop, can't turn back now.

I wind my way to the back through the kitchen, my heart in my throat, my palms slick with sweat. That's when I notice it. Sitting on the workstation is an envelope. A crisp, white rectangle, perched atop a gleaming silver pedestal. I take a few steps toward it, dropping the long train of my dress behind me. My name is scrawled across the front. I sit my phone down on the steel table, the clanking sound echoing through the silence.

With shaking hands, I pick up the envelope, my fingers

fumbling with the flap. Inside, there's a single sheet of paper, the words carefully written out in stark, black ink.

I TOLD YOU, EITHER CALL OFF THE WEDDING OR I WILL.

I stare at the message, my mind reeling. But before I can even begin to process the implications, I feel a sudden, sharp pain at the back of my head. A blinding, white-hot pain that sends me stumbling forward, face down on the table. My vision blurs at the edges, the kitchen I know so well suddenly turning upside down.

I try to scream, to cry out for help, but my voice won't cooperate, my throat closing up tightly. I feel myself falling, my body crumpling to the ground like a marionette with its strings cut. Out of the corner of my eye, I see someone. A woman with cold blue eyes and pale blonde hair.

It couldn't be...

And then, there's nothing. Just the weight of my wedding dress and the cold, hard floor beneath my cheek.

PART 2

CHARLOTTE

CHAPTER THIRTY-TWO

ONE YEAR EARLIER

When I was a little girl, my mother would always say, "Remember, Charlotte, a smile is a lady's most enchanting accessory." It was an antiquated thought, from a soon-to-be-forgotten time when women were seen as accessories to men and not individuals in their own right. But to my mother, it was important. So much so, that if I didn't have a smile plastered on my face, she would reach over and pinch the soft flesh on the back of my tiny right arm. When the bruises grew too dark, she'd switch to the left.

So, I learned to smile, *a lot.*

I must admit, that lesson has been quite useful in my daily life. Maintaining a constant smile on your face is the perfect disguise for hiding your true emotions, a skill I almost constantly employ. So, as Tucker pulls the car to a stop in front of the small bakery on Main Street, I keep an unwavering smile on my face, even though the shop is shabbier than I anticipated. The storefront appears tiny, with a hand-made pink and white awning fluttering in the wind. Elsa, the expensive wedding planner my mother insisted we hire for the big day, raved about this place as the next "big thing." She wanted to create something extravagant and innovative for our nuptials and position me as a trendsetter in the South.

My mother practically salivated at the idea of my wedding setting new trends. I nearly roll my eyes at the thought. Mother, the epitome of old-fashioned tradition and manners, suddenly fancies herself a trendsetter. It's like watching a grandparent trying to navigate TikTok. But of course, Mother adores Elsa. Her over-the-top ideas are the perfect vehicle to flaunt her wealth and dazzle the country club ladies.

Tucker opens the car door and takes my hand as I step out. I give myself a moment and smooth out the white linen jumpsuit, flicking off a few pieces of lint. I adjust my pale blue Birkin bag on my arm just so, wrapping the silk scarf around the handle. Tucker waits patiently as I throw my shoulders back, sending my long blonde hair over my shoulder.

As I take his arm, my mind drifts to the early days with Tucker. Of course he checks all the boxes—gorgeous, wealthy, respectable family—but it was his kindness that truly won me over. The way he listened intently when I spoke, his gentle touches, the thoughtful gestures—all so different from the cold criticism I'd grown up with. For once, I felt seen, appreciated. It was intoxicating, this feeling of being valued for who I was, not just how I looked or what I achieved. It was easy to fall madly in love with him.

Of course, that was a few years ago. Now things are *different*.

"Ready?" he says, attempting a smile to conceal his impatience.

I give him a nod of my chin, and we walk toward the bakery. It's been a year since the engagement, and things have changed between us. I don't know if it's the wedding or my overbearing mother or something else. He's been...distant.

In fact, last night, when I slipped under the covers naked next to him, he was already asleep. Or he was *pretending* to be asleep. It's been an all-too-common occurrence lately—he works late, stumbles home, and drifts off before I can even attempt to snuggle up next to him. It's as if he's become a stranger, his mind constantly preoccupied. And whenever I dare to bring up our impending nuptials, he responds with an exasperated roll of his eyes and a litany of complaints about the mounting expenses.

We step up to the small but brightly painted front door. Well, at the very least, he should be happy with the choice of bakery. Anything this tiny can't cost much more than a dime.

A tacky little silver bell rings as we step inside the front door. The overwhelming scent of sugar permeates the air. I gave up sugar years ago because, as Mother says, a Southern woman must always watch her figure. Surveying the hodge-podge of mismatched furniture in a kaleidoscope of pastels, I can't help but think that this place is little more than a fancy cupcake stand. But I keep my thoughts to myself, not wanting to ruffle any feathers. After all, Elsa is the best wedding planner on the East Coast, and if she says this is our place, then it is.

"Welcome to Couture Cakes!" a voice chimes from behind the counter. I turn to see a petite redhead with a flour-dusted apron and a bright smile. It's the first time we've met in person and I'm slightly taken aback by her appearance. *She's gorgeous.*

"Reese, darling, it's an absolute pleasure to finally meet you in person," I say, stepping forward and grasping her hands.

"Likewise, Miss Spencer," she replies.

Well, aren't you just a stereotypical baker, I think, taking in her perky demeanor and girl-next-door good looks. My eyes wander to a framed photo on the wall—a younger version of her, grinning widely next to an elderly woman. Ten bucks says that's Grandma, and they spent every weekend elbow-deep in cookie dough. But again, I bite my tongue, instead letting my eyes dance around the room for show.

"Oh my goodness, Reese! This place is an absolute dream," I say.

Reese's cheeks flush with pride. "Thank you so much, Miss Spencer," she says. "I've poured my heart and soul into every inch of this place. It means the world to hear you say that."

I hold back a skeptical look. "Please, call me Charlotte. We're practically family now, aren't we?"

"Of course, Charlotte," she replies, gesturing for us to follow her into a small room. A table has been laid out with cake samples, more mismatched china, and a few teacups. "I've prepared a special selection of cakes for you to sample, each one a labor of love."

Labor of love? I nearly gag, wondering if the green juice I had for breakfast might make its way up my throat. As we take our seats, I notice the way Tucker's eyes linger on Reese, his gaze traveling over her slender arms and red hair. My stomach turns into knots. With the divide widening between us, the last thing I need right now is for someone to turn his head.

As the tasting progresses, things only get worse. He laughs at her jokes, leans in close to whisper in her ear, even reaches out to brush a stray bit of frosting from her cheek.

What the hell is going on here?

Maybe I'm overreacting. And why shouldn't I? Tucker and I haven't had sex in weeks, and I'm starting to wonder if he's getting cold feet about the wedding. The thought sends a jolt of panic down my spine. No, that would be a *nightmare.* If he called off the wedding, I'd never recover from the heartbreak, the shame, and most especially, my mother's disappointment.

I force myself to keep my composure, to play the role of the blushing bride-to-be even as my blood boils beneath the surface. I make a show of *ooh*ing and *aah*ing over each cake, pretending to savor every bite even as the sweetness turns to ash on my tongue.

"Oh, Tucker, darling, what do you think of the lemon chiffon?" I ask, my voice syrupy sweet. "Isn't it just divine?"

But Tucker barely glances in my direction, his eyes still glued to Reese's face. "Hmm? Oh, yeah, it's great," he says distractedly, waving a dismissive hand in my direction. "What do you think, Reese? You're the expert here."

Reese just laughs, her eyes sparkling. "Well, I may be biased, but I think the lemon chiffon is one of our best-sellers," she says, leaning forward conspiratorially. "It's light and airy, with just the right amount of tartness to balance out the sweetness."

Just as I'm about to lose my temper over their overt flirta-tion, the doorbell chimes again with that irritating ding. I turn to look over my shoulder and see none other than Mother gliding through the door. My jaw clenches as I recognize the suit she's wearing—the exact Chanel ensemble

I splurged on last month. Of course she'd swoop in wearing it today, a subtle reminder that whatever I have, she can take and wear better.

I jump up from my seat and smooth my white linen jumpsuit, tucking a loose strand of hair behind my ear. Tucker stands as well, his jaw slightly agape. Reese looks between the two of us, her face a mask of confusion. And then she sees my mother sashaying toward us, her designer heels barely making a sound on the hardwood floor, and she stands as well.

Leave it to Mother—her timing is always impeccable.

CHAPTER THIRTY-THREE

"Mother," I say. "I—uh—didn't know you were joining us."

"Don't stutter, dear. It's unattractive," she says, waving me off with her freshly manicured hand. My cheeks burn slightly. The large diamond on her ring finger catches the light, casting tiny rainbows across the room. Even after Father died nearly ten years ago, she still wears it every day. "I just wanted to pop in and see how my favorite couple are doing with their cake tasting."

She holds out her hands to Tucker, her immaculately styled blonde hair not moving an inch as she leans in. "So good to see you, my dear," she says, air-kissing him on each cheek. Tucker stiffens almost imperceptibly, but I know him well enough to sense his discomfort.

Reese, ever the gracious host, works her way around the table. "I'll get another place setting for you, Mrs. Spencer," she says, her smile not quite reaching her eyes.

As soon as Reese leaves the room, the atmosphere shifts. The air feels thick with tension, the silence broken only by the delicate clink of my mother fingering a pink and gold teacup.

"Now, Charlotte, darling," my mother begins, her voice dripping with false sweetness. "I've been thinking about the floral arrangements for the reception. Don't you think we should add some more orchids? They're so elegant, and they would really elevate the whole affair."

I can feel Tucker's gaze boring into me, his jaw clenched tight. The orchids are nearly fifty dollars per head. We just discussed the budget the other night, and I know he's already stretched thin with the expenses. The last thing we need is my mother adding more extravagant touches.

"Mother, I think the arrangements are lovely as they are," I say carefully, trying to keep my tone light. "Tucker and I are happy with what we've chosen."

My mother's eyes narrow, her lips pursing in disapproval. "But surely, Tucker wants the best for his bride, don't you, dear?" she says, turning her attention to him. "After all, you are the one paying for this little soirée."

Tucker's face flushes, his hand gripping his fork so tightly his knuckles turn white. I can practically feel the anger radiating off him, but he says nothing, just glares at me from across the table.

Even though it's traditionally the bride's family who bears the financial burden of the wedding, Tucker offered to pay. The proper Southern response should have been to deny his offer, but our situation is unique. My mother and I live off the Spencer family trust, money that has been passed down for generations. But when my father died, we made a shocking discovery—my father was terrible with money. Due to a string of risky investments, and just plain bad luck, the bulk of the estate was gone. We lived lavishly off my father's life insurance policy for years, burning through our inheritance as if there was no limit. But there was a limit, a fact my mother woefully ignored.

Despite our dire situation, she continues spending with reckless abandon, as if money grows on peach trees. Her cavalier attitude infuriates me. "We are Spencers, dear, we deserve the very best," she always proclaims, blind to the fact that her choices have brought us to the brink of ruin.

So when Tucker proposed, my mother saw an opportunity to get the financial help she needed—from my husband. She instructed me to keep our situation hush-hush until the ink has dried on our wedding certificate. I've done as she told me, although the guilt over hiding this from Tucker has been gnawing at me. But that isn't the only reason—if Tucker knew how bad our finances are, I worry he might not go through with the wedding.

After the proposal, Tucker suddenly became more distant. I mostly ignored the coolness in his affection and doubled my efforts to be a better fiancée. It made things manageable between us. But the last few months? It's like I've been walking on splintered glass. And each one of my mother's demands brings with it a fresh crack in our relationship.

I recall the fight he and I had a few days ago, where things got heated. "Your mother needs to butt out of our wedding," Tucker had said, his voice tight with frustration. "If she wants to add expenses to our wedding, she can pay for those additions herself."

I tried to defend her, to explain that she just wanted the best for us, that asking her to pay would be offensive, making things more tense between us. Tucker wasn't having it. "She wants the best for herself, Charlotte. Can't you see that?

Everything always has to be about her, about keeping up appearances."

"And your parents aren't doing the same? Trying to keep up appearances?"

This comment infuriated him, and we ended up sleeping in separate beds that night. Now, sitting here, with my mother's expectations bearing down on us, I wonder if Tucker was right. It's more than just her tastes and preferences dominating our lives. It's about control, and I'm starting to think he sees it too.

I glance at Tucker, noticing the tightness around his jaw as my mother prattles on about floral arrangements. It's the same look he had when she "suggested" we change our honeymoon destination, or when she casually mentioned she'd already picked out the preschool for our future children. Maybe that's why he's been pulling away from me, canceling dinner dates and staying late at the office. He sees a future where every decision is dominated by my mother.

Reese returns, breaking the uncomfortable silence with her bright chatter about the different cake flavors and fillings. But even as I smile and nod, pretending to be engrossed in the decision, I can't shake the feeling of unease that settles in the pit of my stomach. I glance at Tucker, hoping to catch his eye, to share a moment of solidarity. But he's staring down at his plate, his expression unreadable. I feel a pang of fear in my chest.

The rest of the tasting passes in a blur, my mind too consumed with the distance between Tucker and me to focus on anything else. I let Mother take the lead on sketching out the cake design with Reese, while Tucker and I sit back and watch. By the time we're finished, I feel heavy with exhaustion, the faux smile causing my cheeks to ache.

"Well, this has been just lovely," I say, my voice dripping with false sincerity as we gather our things to leave. "Thank you so much for your time, Reese. We'll be in touch."

We say goodbye to Mother, who makes a quick exit, saying something about a meeting for her new charity event. As we step out into the bright Somerville sunshine, Tucker's hand rests lightly on the small of my back. He's there next to me, touching me, but he might as well be a thousand miles away. And despite the smile I bear on my face, I can't shake the nagging feeling that something's finally broken between us.

CHAPTER THIRTY-FOUR

"Ouch!" I yelp as the tennis ball slams into my side. Glancing across the court, I catch Monica's brief smirk before it morphs into fake concern.

"Oh, Charlotte, dear, I am so sorry. I thought you were ready," she coos.

Of course you did. Trying to conceal my annoyance, I offer a curt nod, saying nothing as the match continues. It's Thursday, which means another thrilling day at the Kessler Tennis Club—the social nexus for anyone who's anyone within twenty miles of Somerville.

As for Monica hitting me with the ball? Let's face it, she did that on purpose. Monica's been trying to bully me since high school when I blossomed early and she...well, didn't. Her resentment has fueled years of petty acts. Like the time she "accidentally" spilled punch on my homecoming dress, or when she started that vicious rumor about me and the chemistry teacher. All our friends turned against me for a while over that. Even now, it's hard to think of those times, of how I dealt with the pressure from them and my mother's constant criticism. It was Dad who helped me through it, got me into therapy when he found out I was cutting. I imagine I can feel the scars on my thighs itch when I think about them now. But years of therapy have helped me develop healthier ways to process my emotions.

So when Monica tosses out her backhanded compliments about my wedding plans or makes not-so-subtle digs about my figure, I can let it roll off my back. Well, *mostly*. Lately I feel like I've been stumbling back to my high school ways. Among all the stress about the wedding, the urge to cut myself has returned.

For now, I channel my frustrations into winning the match. My partner, Cara Dawson, and I have dominated today's doubles game—much to Monica's poorly concealed chagrin. I've always been a better player than Monica, and she knows it. I pull out a ball tucked under my pale blue tennis skirt and serve the final shot, which Monica leaps for and misses. She lands on the ground with a loud thud.

That's karma, Monica. I don't try to conceal the tiny smile on my face. A few minutes later, the four of us saunter over to the water station, and Monica sidles up next to me.

"Great match today, Charlotte."

"You too, Monica," I acknowledge coolly, sipping my cucumber water.

"So," Cara chirps, flinging her light blonde ponytail over her shoulder as she stands next to us, "did ya'll hear who Zach Caldwell is dating?"

My ears perk up involuntarily. Zach and I dated from our senior year in high school all the way through college. Everyone thought we would get married, that we were the perfect couple. But when he finally popped the question, I said no. I just couldn't marry him; it didn't feel right. Zach was crushed, of course. I second-guessed my decision to end things for months afterward.

That is, until that first date with Tucker. Then it all made sense. I could never have loved Zach the way I do Tucker. But I still keep tabs on Zach. *Just in case.*

"Oh yes, he's been seeing that little baker, Reese Montgomery, for a few months. I heard he's completely smitten."

I nearly choke on my water. *Zach's dating Reese?* It's like a punch to the gut. Not only has Reese been flirting with my fiancé, but now she's dating my ex-boyfriend too?

"Are you okay, Charlotte?" Monica asks, her eyes gleaming.

"Yes, I'm just fine," I manage, my voice steadier than I feel.

Monica sets down her glass. "You know, I always thought Zach would never get over you. But it turns out all it took was a little cupcake for him to move on."

Cara rolls her eyes. "Very funny, Monica."

"I think that's great," I say, putting down my glass. "I've always wanted Zach to be happy."

Okay, it's not a *complete* lie. I do want Zach to be happy, but I did always like the idea that he carried a candle for me, even after we broke up. It was comforting, in a way, to think that someone out there still pined for me.

"See you all next week!" Cara says, breaking my thoughts. The four of us take her cue to split and head for the parking lot. As I settle into my car, I keep replaying the words over and over in my head.

Zach is dating Reese.

I should be relieved, right? If she's dating Zach that means she has no interest in my fiancé. And with the way

Tucker has been "dropping in" to the bakery, I was beginning to get concerned.

A FEW HOURS LATER, I step into my kitchen and freeze. There, on the counter, sits a white box emblazoned with the gold "Couture Cakes" logo. I stifle a groan. It feels like I can't escape Reese's presence; this woman has somehow managed to weasel her way into every aspect of my life—even my new kitchen.

Tucker appears beside me, planting a kiss on my cheek. His face brightens with a smile that doesn't quite ease my tension.

"I thought you might like a little treat," he says warmly. "I know things have been stressful lately with all the wedding planning."

I force a smile in return, lifting the lid to peer inside. I suppose he meant it as a peace offering after our latest argument, but the sight of the perfectly frosted cupcakes only makes my stomach churn.

"Thank you," I say, my voice carefully neutral. "Did you pick them up on your way home from work?"

Tucker nods, his gaze flickering away from mine for just a moment. "Yeah, I had a meeting downtown and figured I'd stop by the shop. Reese mentioned that she'd been experimenting with some new flavors."

There it is again, that name. Reese. The way it rolls off his tongue so easily, like it's been on the forefront of his mind all day. Jealousy flares in my chest, hot and sharp.

"How thoughtful of her," I say, my tone just a touch too bright. "I'm sure she's thrilled to have such a loyal customer."

Tucker frowns, his brow furrowing in confusion. "What's that supposed to mean?"

I sigh, pushing the box away from me. "Nothing, Tucker. It's just...don't you think it's a little strange, how much time you've been spending at the bakery lately? I mean, we've already chosen our wedding cake. What else is there to discuss?"

His eyes flash with anger. "For goodness' sake, Charlotte, it's just cupcakes. I'm just trying to support a local small business. Why do you have to read into everything?"

I can feel my own temper rising, the resentment that's been simmering under the surface for weeks now threatening to boil over. "Because every time I turn around, you're talking about her. Reese this, Reese that. If I didn't know better, I'd think you were more excited about the damn cake than you are about marrying me."

Tucker slams his hand down on the counter, making me jump. "That's ridiculous, and you know it. I love you, Charlotte. I wouldn't be putting up with all this wedding crap, not to mention your mother, if I didn't."

His words sting like a slap across the face. *Putting up with.* Like our wedding is some kind of burden, a cross he has to bear. Tears well up in my eyes, but I blink them back, refusing to let him see how much he's hurt me.

"Fine," I say, my voice cold and clipped. "I'm going to bed."

"Charlotte—" he says, reaching out to me.

I turn on my heel and stalk out of the room, leaving Tucker standing there with his well-intentioned box of cupcakes. I know he'll come climbing into bed later, apologizing. Maybe this time, *I'll* be the one pretending to sleep. When I take my first step on the staircase, exhaustion hits me like a wave—not just physical fatigue from tennis, but a bone-deep weariness from constantly maintaining this façade of perfection.

The wedding is barely a week away, and it feels like everything is unraveling at the seams. Is this normal? Do all brides-to-be feel like their fiancés can barely tolerate them? Like they're one minor setback away from a complete breakdown?

I reach the bedroom door and briefly turn my head back toward the kitchen. I can't shake the idea that Tucker is hiding something from me. *I can feel it.*

CHAPTER THIRTY-FIVE

"Excuse me," says the woman behind the shoe counter, her voice tinged with hesitation. "Ma'am?"

I snap back to attention. "Yes?"

I realize I have zoned out, staring at the wall of carefully arranged shoes behind the counter. The lack of sleep is catching up to me, fogging my normally sharp brain. I barely slept last night, tossing and turning as flashes of red hair invaded my dreams. *Reese.* She's all I can think about. Dating my ex-boyfriend, flirting with my husband.

I also can't shake that annoying feeling that Tucker has a thing for her. I chew on the inside of my cheek, trying to dispel the thought. He said it last night: *I'm marrying you, Charlotte. I love you.* But it just doesn't feel like the words are enough to convince me.

When I woke up alone, I realized the only thing that would make me feel any better was some retail therapy. I still needed shoes for Friday's rehearsal dinner, so I decided to head into Charleston. So here I am staring into space as the saleswoman wraps up the most beautiful pair of strappy pearlescent heels I could find. I should be delighted, the rush of a new purchase flowing through my veins. Instead, I'm staring at the wall, my eyes glazed over.

"I'm sorry, your credit card has been declined," she explains, her big, brown almond eyes meeting mine apologetically.

What? That can't be right. My stomach clenches. "Run it again," I demand, my voice tight. I glance over my shoulder at the woman waiting behind me. She's looking down at her phone, but I know she heard everything.

"I'm sorry, it's been declined again," the clerk says softly.

Heat rises to my cheeks. "Fine," I say, trying to keep my voice steady. "There must be a problem. I'm sure it's just... I'll have to call my bank." I open my bag with trembling hands. Thankfully, I have just enough cash to pay for the shoes. I place a couple of hundred-dollar bills on the counter, my face burning with embarrassment. I keep my eyes downcast as I rush out the front door.

As soon as I'm out on the street and out of earshot, I call my mother. We share a credit card tied to our family trust, so she must know why I'd be declined.

"Mother?" I say as soon as she picks up, my voice strained.

"Yes, dear, what is it? I'm in the middle of—"

I cut her off, my words tumbling out in a rush. "My credit card was just declined at the boutique. What's going on? Why was it declined?"

My mother lets out a nervous laugh. "Oh dear, don't worry about it. Listen, I'm having lunch with Lucinda Caldwell. You know, Zach's mother?"

I roll my eyes. Of course, Mother loves the Caldwell family and continues to have lunch with Lucinda once a month, even though Zach and I broke up years ago. Clearly now is not the time to discuss our financial troubles. We don't need Lucinda spreading any gossip about the Spencer family trust issues.

"Yes, I know who she is, Mother. Tell her I said hello," I say, trying to keep the irritation out of my voice. "Call me as soon as you're done, okay?"

I thrust the phone back into my bag and head to my car, my mind racing. Something's up with Mother. As if the stress of the wedding isn't enough, she seems to be stretching our finances to the brink of bankruptcy. *Yet again.* I bite my lip. I need to get this wedding over with so I can have some breathing room. I've been under her thumb my whole life, the trust fund hanging over my head like a dark cloud. Tucker has already agreed to give me a generous monthly allowance, so I won't need the family money anyway. She can have it, to spend how she wishes.

And if Mother spends everything we inherit? She's on her own.

The frustration with my mother churns in my stomach, and I realize I've hardly eaten anything since morning. I decide to stop at Gordon's Gourmet just outside of Somerville to grab a quick salad and an iced tea. I park my car half a block down the street and walk up to the front door of the deli. A man holds the door open for me, and I slip inside, my eyes fixed on the display case of food. But something catches my attention from across the room—a flash of red hair, just like in my dreams last night.

I look over to the corner of the deli and stop cold. There, sitting at a tiny bistro table and leaning toward each other, are *Tucker and Reese*. Their knees are practically touching under the table and their heads are bent in conversation.

He's smiling at her, that same easy grin that used to be reserved only for me. And she's laughing, her hand resting lightly on his arm in a gesture that's far too familiar for my liking.

My vision blurs with tears. *They look like a couple.* Like two people in love, sharing a secret joke. I stumble back from the counter, my breath coming in short, sharp gasps.

Why is he here? Having lunch with her?

I can't let them see me, so I turn on my heel and barrel toward the door. When I reach the sidewalk, I dare a glance over my shoulder. They are still there, talking to each other as if I don't exist. *This can't be happening.* My breath becomes ragged, and my heart pounds so hard that it feels like it may come out my ears.

He can't be cheating on me. Not days before our wedding.

No. No. No.

I race to my car, desperate for a place to hide. Once inside, I press my forehead on the leather of my steering wheel. Maybe I just imagined it. I mean, I barely slept last night. And I haven't been taking my anti-anxiety meds because I want to get pregnant as soon as the wedding is over. In fact, I hoped it would happen on our honeymoon. My doctor said it was okay, as long as I felt I could handle the stress.

But this? This is more than stress. This is my life being turned upside down. I feel myself panting again, and a sharp pain sears my chest. I turn on the car and blast the air conditioning. I try to take some breaths—four seconds in, hold seven seconds, eight seconds out.

Nothing helps.

I try to convince myself that it's all in my head, that I'm

reading too much into an innocent interaction, but I know deep down that I'm not. That the connection between Tucker and Reese is real, and it's been growing right under my nose. *How could I have been so blind?*

I sit behind the wheel, my tears flowing freely now, my body racked with sobs. *This can't be how it ends*, I think, my heart breaking into a million pieces. I can't lose him, not like this.

Suddenly I spot the two of them leaving the deli. Tucker opens the door for her and she glides out, a wide grin on her face. She tips her head to the side as they chat on the sidewalk. Tucker leans in and gives her a kiss on the cheek. Even from behind the glass of my car, I see her blush. It's written all over her face. *She's in love with him.*

I lean down in my car, careful to hide my face from view. Once the two of them are gone, I sit back up. I'm spiraling now, and my head feels light. Tucker has been so distant... and now I know why. It's all because of *her.*

My eyes linger on the glove box of my car. I keep a set of razors in there, just in case. I mean, I never really planned on using them, but having them right within reach and *not* using them makes me feel like I'm in control. But any control I felt before is gone.

I reach over to the glove box with a shaky hand and pull out the little pink envelope. Inside is a shiny set of flat metal razors. As the light catches on the silver metal, I think of Tucker, *my Tucker*, in the arms of another woman. And I know it's my fault. *I wasn't enough.*

Despite looking the part, acting the part, giving him every bit of love I had, it wasn't enough. I stare at the blade. The urge to hurt myself, to punish myself for not being enough, is too strong to resist.

I pull up my skirt and press the blade on the middle of my thigh, watching with detached fascination as the blood wells up in thin, crimson lines. The pain is sharp and immediate, a welcome distraction from the agony in my heart. *I deserve this,* I think as I make another cut, and then another. I deserve to suffer for being so stupid, so blind.

After a few minutes, I let out a huge sigh of relief. *There, that's better.* I wipe the blade with a tissue and tuck it back into the envelope. It's just enough to take the edge off. But as the initial rush fades, a wave of shame crashes over me. Years of resistance, undone in a moment of weakness. I suddenly feel sick, disgusted with myself. *How could I fall back into this old habit so easily?*

Despite the conflicting emotions, I force myself to start thinking about my next steps. If I'm going to save this wedding, I need to act carefully. I push aside the feelings of self-loathing and try to focus on what's ahead. I'm going to need help from someone I can trust. And that's a short list. I pull up my phone and reluctantly dial my mother.

"Hi, Mom," I say, my voice coming out like a squeak.

"Hello, dear. Is this about the credit card? Because—"

"No, Mom, it's—" I say, interrupting her. The calm I felt only a moment ago begins to evaporate. Before I can stop myself, I feel the tears coming again.

"Oh, my child, what is it?"

"It's Tucker," I say between sobs. "I think he's having an affair."

CHAPTER THIRTY-SIX

Mother and I met at her house shortly after I called her. For once, my cold mother was sympathetic. She patted me on the back and spoke softly in my ear. Then the two of us came up with a plan. I needed proof that Tucker was cheating on me, before I jumped to conclusions. Once I knew for sure he was cheating, then we would move forward with the second part of our plan.

I still wanted to marry Tucker, so it had to be done *carefully*.

Back in my kitchen, I feel a little silly as I open my laptop and type "how to catch your cheating fiancé" into the search bar. *Desperate times call for desperate measures, I suppose.* The internet, of course, is full of useful information —how to set traps, how to install tracking applications on phones. I'm deep into an article about hidden cameras when my phone buzzes.

It's a text from Tucker:

Working late tonight, babe. Don't wait up.

I stare at the message for a beat longer. Half of me wants to laugh, the other half wants to throw my phone across the room and watch it shatter against the wall. It's going to be almost too easy catching the two of them together. I still can't believe it—only two days until the wedding, and he's "working late." I know exactly what it means.

He's with her. *Reese*.

Then it hits me—all this research is unnecessary. The solution is right at my fingertips. Tucker and I share logins for each other's cell phone accounts. With trembling hands, I open the "Find My Phone" app, and there he is, a blinking dot on the screen.

I take a deep breath, steadying myself, and swipe open my phone to look at where he is now—near the Charleston Place Hotel of all places. Which means they're probably getting a room together, so they can shack up on the hotel's famous silky white sheets. A menacing visual of the two of them naked in bed, twisted in a moment of ecstasy, rattles my brain. I nearly lose my lunch.

Focus, Charlotte.

I shake my head and breathe, dispelling the thought. What I need to do is focus on tonight. I should have just enough time to change before heading out the door. I slip on a pair of black leggings, a baggy black hoodie, and a black cap. To make sure he doesn't recognize my blonde hair, I tuck a chin-length brown wig under my cap.

I glance at myself in the hallway mirror just before stepping out to the garage. I bite my lip, doubt creeping in. I've wiped all the makeup off my face, and the hollows under my eyes are dark and deep, and my skin looks pale. There's no question this disguise will work—I don't think my own mother would recognize me from a distance. But it all feels a little bit ridiculous. *Has it really come to this?* Am I really disguising myself to go check if my fiancé is cheating on me just days before our wedding?

Before I can break down into tears, I grab my keys off the table and bolt for the door. I set my phone on the dashboard of my car, keeping the blinking location just within view. It looks like he's past the hotel and is moving further west. My mind races with possibilities. *Are they leaving the hotel together? Heading to dinner? Did they already have sex in the room and now they're hungry?* The thought nearly makes me sick. I glance at the glove box, thinking again of my razors. But I won't have time for that. *I need to stay focused.*

I try to clear my head and focus on the traffic lights, the lines on the road, the pedestrian signs—anything to keep me from thinking about Reese and Tucker together. I'm so focused on not thinking about what's happening that I almost miss it when I realize I'm heading directly toward Tucker's warehouse in Charleston.

I chew on my lip, confusion setting in. This isn't what I expected. What if he actually is working late tonight? Normally his warehouse crews are off duty by now, so it's strange that he'd be driving to the warehouse so late at night.

I suddenly feel foolish. I tug my cap down further onto my head as I weave in and out of traffic. I consider turning back for a moment, but what if she's here? What if the two of them are meeting here? The thought of them in his office isn't that far-fetched. They could easily rendezvous here; he has a large office with a bathroom and cot in the back.

I decide to forge ahead, since I've already come this far.

I manage to spot Tucker's SUV up ahead, about three cars in front of me. I hang back, making sure he doesn't see my car. A few minutes later, I see him turn off the street toward the warehouse gates. I drive past, giving him plenty of time to park before I find a spot down the street. I grab a flashlight out of my bag, along with my phone and a pair of binoculars.

My heart beats rapidly as I creep through the darkness. The shipyard is large, with rows upon rows of shipping containers stacked high, creating a mazelike layout. Cranes loom overhead, and the salty smell of the harbor fills the air. Tucker's warehouse has security and cameras, but I've been here a few times and he's shown me the lay of the land. I know there's a door in the back that I can slip into without being seen, by the water.

My hands shake as I lift the metal latch and slip through the door. I carefully make my way through the dimly lit paths between containers, staying alert for any signs of movement or voices. I glance warily at the security cameras peppered around the property. Suddenly the brown wig and cap don't feel so foolish.

My heart races as I creep closer. A small pebble skitters beneath my foot, and I freeze, holding my breath. But the constant whooshing of the wind from the ocean and the gentle lapping of water against the docks mask the sound. Relief washes over me, and I press on, grateful for the sound cover.

I spot Tucker in the corner standing next to an open shipping container. He's speaking with a man dressed in a reflective vest, carrying a clipboard. I weave in and out of the containers until I'm about ten feet away, just within earshot.

"This shipment's better than the last," a voice says. Not Tucker's.

"They're getting good," Tucker replies. "Soon, no one will be able to tell the difference—if they even still can."

Around the corner, Tucker is standing with his back to me, examining what appears to be a Louis Vuitton Neverfull bag. I glance around at the stacks and stacks of boxes. Louis Vuitton bags are made in France; however, all of these boxes are stamped with "Made in China."

"How many we got?" the other man asks.

"Two hundred Gucci, one hundred and fifty Louis Vuitton," Tucker says. "Street value close to one million."

My breath catches in my throat. I can hardly believe what I'm seeing. These are *counterfeit* bags. Tucker is selling counterfeit bags. I feel my breath quicken. This is not what I expected, not what I came here for. I thought I'd find him with Reese, get the proof I need to confront him.

Now? I'm not sure what to do. I feel my mouth hanging open, staring at what feels like a train wreck. The fight or flight part of my brain suddenly clicks on and a dozen questions start running through my mind. Should I run? Should I go up and ask Tucker what all this is about? Is his fortune built on lies? On crime? Counterfeit goods are illegal— extremely illegal. If Tucker got caught doing this...

The last thought tumbles around in my brain for a few seconds before I realize the opportunity in front of me. I hit the record button on my phone and take a video, then photos. After capturing about a dozen or so shots, I tuck my phone back into my pocket.

Tucker is moving now, turning his body toward me. That's my cue. I quickly step back into the shadows and look for my exit. Once I hear the two of them walk away, I run back to my car, never stopping to look over my shoulder. I can see a few cameras ahead of me, but if they record me, they'll never see who it is. It's too dark, and the black clothes should blend into the shadows. I'm just ten yards away from the back gate.

A dog's bark pierces the night air, distant but unmistakable. My heart leaps into my throat, and I break into a cold sweat. Images of Tucker's snarling guard dogs flash through my mind, their teeth bared and eyes gleaming in the darkness. I pick up my pace, my breath coming in short, panicked gasps.

When I'm finally settled in the leather seat of my car, I let out a long sigh. *I made it.* I don't take time to dwell on what just happened. I turn on the ignition and pull onto the road. As I make my way back home, reality sinks in.

My soon-to-be husband is a criminal.

Everything we have is built on lies. The sprawling mansion with its manicured gardens. My closet overflowing with Chanel and Gucci. Those lavish vacations to St. Tropez and Bali. All of it, tainted. I rub my forehead, trying to decide what to do next.

Should I call off the wedding? Should I call the police? I can only imagine the look on Mother's face when she finds out my fiancé was arrested for fraud. She'd never recover from the shame, and neither would I.

I debate whether or not to call her, but this wasn't a part of our plan. I bite my lip. No, telling Mother is out of the question. I need someone to talk to. To help me figure this out. I quickly dial Cara. Her husband is a criminal attorney. He's just out of law school, but I'm sure he knows something I could do.

"Hello?" she says. She sounds tired, like she was just about to fall asleep.

"Cara, it's Charlotte."

"Oh, hi. What's up, Char? Is everything okay?"

"Yes...I mean no. It's about Tucker. I just found out something about him and I—" Just as I am about to tell her the whole story, I see Tucker's car at the intersection in front of me.

Crap! I can't let him see me.

"Charlotte?"

"Listen, sorry I bothered you," I say, recovering. "I'll talk to you tomorrow, okay?"

"Sure—"

I hang up before she has a chance to say goodbye. I slam on the breaks and peel down a side street before Tucker sees me. Once his taillights are out of sight, I steer my car into a U-turn.

I stare off into the darkness and shake my head. It's a sign. Calling Cara was not the right move. Despite the growing chasm between Tucker and me and the new revelation that he is, in fact, a criminal, *I still love him.*

I pull over to the side of the road, my thoughts racing. *Should I be telling Cara? My mother? Anyone?* If Cara tells her husband, Tucker might actually go to jail. The thought makes my stomach lurch. No, I can't let that happen. Finding out how flawed he really is seems to set the scales even between us. I've suspected he wasn't perfect for a while now—why else would I have come out tonight to catch him cheating? But this...this is different. It's bigger. And yet, it doesn't change how I feel.

I've never cared about his business or how he makes his money before. In fact, maybe it's better this way. If he's willing to do this for money, maybe I don't need to feel so guilty about needing to marry him for mine. He's just as broken as me, after all. And that makes us perfect for each other. In fact, *I've never wanted to marry him more.*

There's just one thing that stands between the two of us. That annoying little redhead—*Reese.* But she won't be an issue now. Because pretty soon, Tucker won't want to have anything to do with her. Not after he finds out what I have on him.

CHAPTER THIRTY-SEVEN

I pull off the pearl drop earrings I've been wearing all evening and drop them on the glossy granite kitchen countertop in my condo. The earrings have been weighing down my earlobes, leaving a dull ache. Not to mention the beautiful but punishing heels I bought the other day have left deep, angry grooves on my ankles and feet. It feels so good to take both of them off, the cool air soothing my tender skin.

In a way, they mirrored the entire evening—heavy, tight and tense.

Tucker strolls in behind me. He loosens the top button of his shirt with a sigh of relief and peels off his jacket, tossing it over the chair. The rich scent of his cologne lingers in the air. It's been a few months since we've spent time in my condo in downtown Charleston, but here we are. I decided to stay here for the evening before the wedding to keep tradition and not allow Tucker to see his bride before the big day. I plan on running myself a hot bath and having a glass of wine before crawling into bed.

Tucker pulls a beer from the fridge, the glass bottles clinking as he does. He cracks it open with a satisfying hiss. I settle onto the counter stool on the other side of the island and swipe open my phone to look at pictures from the evening. The hashtag #TuckerMarriesCharlotte already has at least a hundred photos on social media. I scroll through them, taking in the smiling faces and raised glasses. Everyone looks so happy, so excited for tomorrow. I see Cara decked out in a gorgeous yellow dress, with her arm looped around her husband. I managed to avoid her for the entire night, which was a feat. I'm not ready to explain the phone call from last night—just yet.

I keep scrolling until I find the lone photo of Tucker and me together. We're standing stiffly side by side, a good six inches of space between us. My smile looks forced, the corners of my mouth tight. Tucker's grin doesn't reach his eyes, which seem distant and unfocused. It's as if we're two strangers awkwardly posed for a picture, not a couple on the eve of their wedding.

Tucker takes a long swig of his beer, the amber liquid catching the soft light, and sets it down on the countertop with a dull thud.

"Charlotte, we need to talk," he says, his voice tight.

That's exactly what I was thinking. I place my phone face down on the counter and pull my hands into my lap. I'm happy to hear what Tucker has to say first. In fact, I can already guess what this is about. *Her.*

"Of course. What is it?" I reply, trying to keep my voice steady.

Tucker shifts his weight, and I can tell by the way his eyes dart around the room that he's nervous. It's an expression I rarely see from him. Tucker is a fairly even-keeled guy;

nothing seems to ruffle his feathers. But clearly, he's on edge now.

"It's about tomorrow..." he begins, his eyes finally leveling with mine. "I think we should call off the wedding."

I shouldn't be surprised. I know I shouldn't be, from the way he stood stiffly through the rehearsal and the distracted way he worked the room all through dinner. It was clear that Tucker was uncomfortable, that he was elsewhere mentally. Not to mention he was pretty cold toward me. I think he kissed me once or twice on the cheek, but for the rest of the night, he barely touched me. I distracted myself by interacting with our other guests, but I kept an eye on him through the entire night.

So I shouldn't be surprised by what he just said, but the words still send a shudder throughout my entire body.

"What are you talking about?" I ask, trying to keep my voice even.

"I'm talking about calling off the wedding, Charlotte," Tucker explains, his voice strained. "I just don't think that we should get married. I..." He pauses, looking down at his hands before turning back to me. "You know we have been fighting for months. We aren't happy. And I don't want to put you through the ceremony and have us just end up divorced a year from now. It's not fair to you. It's not fair to our friends and family, and it's not fair to me."

I take a deep breath, studying him. I stay silent for a few moments, making him wait for my answer, making him wonder. I'm sure he thinks I'm going to implode, to gasp, perhaps even faint right there. But I take every bit of strength in my core, and I stay centered.

"This is about Reese, isn't it?" I accuse, my voice low and controlled. "I saw the two of you together the other day at

Gordon's deli. I know you've been stopping by her place several times a week, supposedly buying cupcakes or making decisions for the wedding. You can't lie to me. I know this is about her. You think you're in love with her, but she's completely wrong for you."

Tucker stares at me, his face paling. Now it's his turn to be silent. I wish I could see or hear what exactly he's thinking. He has a choice—admit this has something to do with her or try to lie his way out of it. Knowing Tucker, he'll try to make it sound like he's doing what's best for me.

But I know better.

"This has nothing to do with Reese," he finally says, his voice strained. "This is about you and me. The last few months? We've barely touched each other. We've barely spoken."

I slam my hand down on the table, the sharp sound echoing through the kitchen as I finally let go of my anger. "*You* haven't touched me. *You* haven't spoken to me," I retort, my voice rising. "I've been trying. I've been doing everything I can, and you act like you're disgusted by me. You won't even touch me anymore. I know it's not because of me—it's because of her."

"It's not because of her, Charlotte!" Tucker shouts, his words exploding out with an anger that makes me shudder. "It's because I'm not in love with you anymore. Don't you get that?"

Tears threaten to start pouring down my face, hot and stinging. I grip my hands into fists as I try to control the pain. I could argue with him at this point. I could tell him that it's not true, that he does love me. But it's useless. He's made up his mind; it's written all over his face. And I can't cancel this wedding. *I won't.*

"We're not going to call it off," I say, my voice trembling despite my efforts to sound strong.

Tucker stares at me, his eyes hard. "I told you, Charlotte. I don't want to marry you. We're going to call off the wedding tomorrow," he insists, his tone leaving no room for argument.

"Oh no, we are not," I say, forcing myself to feel strong even though my heart is shattered. "You will marry me tomorrow because you have no other choice. I know what you've been doing. The Louis Vuitton purses, the Guccis. I know that you have been smuggling illegal counterfeit goods through your warehouse."

I see the shock roll across his features. His eyes grow large, then narrow. I give him a few minutes for the idea to settle in as the two of us face off on either side of the condo kitchen island. Tucker takes another drink of his beer, the glass bottle clinking against his teeth.

"And if you don't marry me tomorrow? I'm going to the police."

"You're insane, Charlotte," he says, his voice a mix of disbelief and anger. "You have no proof. And is this really the way you want to start a marriage? With blackmail?"

I lean forward in my seat, my heart pounding. "That's where you're wrong," I say, my voice steady and cold. "I do have proof. Enough to send you to prison for a very long time."

He's still staring at me, the realization sinking in. *Okay, so I am not one hundred percent sure that's true.* Technically, it's a *little white lie,* but it's enough for the color to drain from Tucker's face.

I lean in close, my voice low and dangerous. "So here's what's going to happen. We're getting married tomorrow.

You'll sign a new prenup—one that's very generous to me. You'll cut ties with Reese. And you'll be the perfect, doting husband."

"And if I don't?"

"You'll need to find a good criminal attorney."

Tucker stares at me for a long moment. I can see the wheels turning, but it's impossible to read him. For a split second, I start to question what I've done. *Have I gone too far?* The thought flashes through my mind, unbidden and unwelcome. A knot forms in my stomach. This isn't how I imagined our wedding eve would be, full of threats and blackmail.

But then I remember the coldness in his touch these past months, the way his eyes lit up when he saw Reese. I think of all the plans we've made, the life we've built together. How can he throw it all away? No, I reassure myself, this is necessary. This is the only way to save us, to save our future. I need this wedding to happen tomorrow. *I'll deal with the rest later.* Once Reese is gone, he'll see clearly again. He'll remember why he fell in love with me in the first place. I can be everything he needs, I know I can. *I just need the chance to prove it.*

Tucker finishes his beer and sets it down.

"Okay," he says finally. "You win."

I straighten my posture and smooth down my dress, trying to regain my composure. The bravado I felt earlier has evaporated, leaving me feeling hollow. Technically, I've won this battle, but victory tastes bitter. The confident woman of moments ago has vanished, replaced by the insecure little girl I thought I'd outgrown—the one perpetually seeking approval. I get up from my seat and walk around the kitchen island. I reach out to him, and he doesn't even flinch.

"I'm sorry it had to be like this, Tucker. I promise I'll make you happy. You'll see."

He raises his chin and walks around me to pick up his jacket. The next few seconds of silence are painful. He pulls on his jacket and begins walking toward the door. I catch up to him, grabbing his left arm. He swings around and looks at me. All the softness has drained out of his eyes. It's not the way he used to look at me, like I was the only girl in the world. It's not the look he gave me after the first time we made love, like I was pure magic.

The look in his eyes right now is that of pure hatred. My heart breaks again.

"I love you," I say, desperate for him to reciprocate.

"I'll see you tomorrow," he says. I let my hand drop. He continues toward the door, then slams it as he leaves. As soon as his steps disappear down the hallway, I fall to the floor and start sobbing. This isn't what I wanted, any of it. I wanted Tucker and me to be happy together. Start a family together. But now it's clear. He hates me.

And there is only one person to blame: *Reese Montgomery.*

PART 3

REESE—PRESENT

CHAPTER THIRTY-EIGHT

My eyes snap open. Panic floods my system as I realize I can't breathe properly. I try to gasp, but my mouth won't open. My heart pounds as I force myself to breathe through my nose. As I do, a potent smell invades my lungs. *Gasoline.*

The scent triggers a coughing fit, and I instinctively try to move my hand to my mouth. It doesn't budge. With a jolt of fear, I realize my hands are bound behind my back. I'm sitting upright, the hard surface beneath me familiar.

Calm down, Reese. I will myself to relax, taking in the gasoline-infused air more slowly. As my breathing steadies, I become aware of a throbbing pain radiating from my right temple down behind my ear. I've been hit—hard.

Confusion mingles with the fear as I try to piece together what's happened. *Why am I here? What happened to my head?* I think, blinking quickly as I try to understand. And it all comes back to me—the threatening messages, the break-in at the shop.

Whoever has been sending those messages is here right now.

I squeeze my eyes shut and breathe deeply, trying to remember what I saw when I got back here. It was just a flash, just for a moment: pale blonde hair, blue eyes.

Charlotte, I think. *It has to be Charlotte.*

The room is dark, but there's just enough light coming from the front of the shop for me to see. *I need to get out of here.* I try to move, but when I do, a sharp pain runs around my wrists. That's when I realize I'm not just on the floor— I'm seated in one of the chairs from the cake tasting room. It's been moved to the kitchen, out of place among the stainless steel counters and baking equipment.

My wrists have been zip-tied to the wooden arms of the chairs with brutal efficiency. The plastic digs into my skin, sending jolts of pain up my arms with every slight move- ment. I can feel the back of the chair pressing against my spine, a lump of fabric bunched up behind me. My ankles are bound to the chair legs so tightly that my heartbeat feels like it's pulsing in my feet. I strain against the bonds, the chair creaking beneath me, but it's useless.

I'm trapped.

My eyes dart around the room, desperate for something that might help me. I'm sitting inside the kitchen of my bakery, a large square room with ovens flanking one wall and metal racks on the other. In the center of the room is a large stainless steel prep station with storage underneath. I glance over to the sink on the opposite wall where a collection of knives are hanging from a strip of magnet against the wall. If only I could reach those knives.

Suddenly, I hear a rustling toward the back of the shop where my office is. I try to scream, to make any kind of noise, but it just sounds like muffled grunting with my mouth covered in what I assume is duct tape.

I look down at my wrists again, struggling against the restraints. That's when I realize I'm still in my wedding dress. My mind reels with the realization. *Wedding dress.*

Tucker! The wedding! The thought hits me like a bolt of lightning. *Oh no, I've got to get out of here. The wedding. Everyone is waiting for me.*

Panic surges through my body as I picture the scene— guests seated in rows, murmuring in confusion. Tucker standing at the altar, his face a mix of worry and disappointment. My mother, his parents, all our friends—everyone we love, waiting. For me. And I'm here, tied to a chair in my own bakery.

This can't be happening.

I struggle harder against the restraints, ignoring the pain as the zip ties cut into my wrists. My muscles strain as I pull against the bonds, but they don't budge. Tears of frustration and fear begin to well up in my eyes. On top of the table I catch the glint of my phone. Its plastic case begins to vibrate, sending a rippling sound through the room. I strain my neck to see the caller. *Tucker.* I try to scream again, as if somehow he could hear me, which is silly. I try to scoot the entire chair forward, but the hem of my dress is tangled up in the chair legs.

A new sound stops me. It sounds like swishing and the splash of liquid splattering on the floor. Then a fresh wave of gasoline assaults my nostrils. My brain processes this and comes to a chilling conclusion: Charlotte's here and she's pouring gasoline all over my shop. Which can only mean one thing—*she's about to set the place on fire.* I struggle harder, trying to break through the zip ties, but it's pointless. I can hardly move. My phone has gone silent.

I try to think and remember what happened when I got

here. Bernie sent me a text message. She said there was smoke, a fire. She said she'd meet me here.

But the shop was empty.

I told the limousine driver to come back once he spoke with Tucker. *I hope he's still coming.* Bernie isn't here, obviously. From what I can hear—footsteps in the next room—it's Charlotte. *And she wants to hurt me.* Seconds crawl by as I listen to the sound of footsteps weaving in and out of each room.

And the awful sound on repeat. *Splash, splash, splash.*

My eyes flit back to my phone lying quietly on the table. If I could get closer, maybe I could work the phone with the tip of my nose. It's worth a shot. I push my shoulders forward and try to stand on my feet. But the ground is slippery, covered in what I presume is the gasoline, so my feet sweep from underneath and I fall to the ground with a hard thud. Pain shoots up my arm and the throbbing on my head gets worse. I moan through the duct tape.

As I hit the ground, I notice something on the floor—the note, the letter that I found when I got here. I try to make noises again, grunting sounds. If Charlotte's really here, maybe she'll actually talk to me. Maybe I can explain what happened and try to understand why she wants to stop the wedding, try to reason with her at least.

I keep making noise, and eventually, the footsteps head my way. The sound of each step is excruciating as I wait; each second is another *click, click, click.* Finally, the person who has been threatening me, who dumped gasoline all over my shop, who slammed me with some blunt object on the side of my head and tied me up, is standing before me.

If my mouth wasn't taped shut, I would have audibly

gasped for air. Instead, I draw a sharp inhale through my nostrils. Because it's not Charlotte standing there in front of me.

It's someone else entirely.

CHAPTER THIRTY-NINE

Amanda Spencer—Charlotte's mother—is standing in the doorway of my bakery kitchen. I blink my eyes several times quickly. *Am I imagining things?* What in the world is she doing here? She looks manic, her eyes wild and large. A large, orange gasoline tank is hanging from her right hand. She's wearing an entirely black ensemble—leggings, sweater, boots—and an unusual amount of jewelry. The bump on my head makes it hard to think clearly, to piece together the puzzle. *Why is she here?*

When her eyes meet mine, I desperately try to gulp for breath. She's glaring at me with what I can only describe as pure hatred.

"Hello, Reese," she says, her voice cold and sharp. She walks across the room, closing the distance between us. When she's about a foot away from me, I flinch, thinking she's going to slap me across the face. Instead she stands on my left side and lifts me with a surprising strength until my chair is upright.

I try to speak, to yell, but she shakes her head, standing in front of me.

"I will take the tape off your mouth, but you have to agree to stay calm." Amanda holds up what looks like a small brass lighter. She flips open the lid. "If you start screaming, I'm going to light this entire place on fire."

As she says that, she looks down at the hem of my dress, which is puddled on the floor. I notice that the entire bottom of the dress has been yellowed from gasoline. I gulp at the realization that with one flick of her lighter my entire dress—and me—will go up in flames. My heart beats so fast I feel like it might crawl up my throat and jump out of my mouth.

I give her a feverish nod, my whole body trembling.

She leans down closer to me, and with one swift motion, rips the duct tape off my mouth. The pain is quick and intense; my entire lower face burns. She tosses the tape on the floor.

"Such a shame to mess up that beautiful makeup," she says, her voice dripping with sarcasm.

"What are you doing here?" I say, my voice coming out weak and raspy.

Amanda turns from me as she speaks, walking back to the end of the prep table where the plastic gasoline can sits. "That's a great question, Reese. What am I doing here?" She turns back to face me. "Well, I tried to tell you to stop the wedding, that Tucker wasn't for you, but you didn't listen. So I had to take matters into my own hands."

I try to think of something to say, but I'm stunned into silence. It was her, the whole time. *Amanda Spencer is the one who's been harassing me.*

"Why?" I croak, unable to muster anything more.

"I wasn't about to let you have the wedding that my daughter had dreamed of. Let you steal her moment from her. So why am I here? To make sure that you don't get to keep what you stole." Her words tumble out in a rush, her eyes gleaming with a manic energy that sends chills down my spine.

My mind races. "What are you talking about? Charlotte left Tucker at the altar. She left him, and now she's gone. He called me the day of the wedding and told me what happened. It was awful what she did to him."

Amanda's eyes flare with something animal. For a moment I think she might jump across the table and strangle me. Instead, she takes a deep breath through her nose and brushes a few wispy strands of hair behind her ear.

I notice that she's wearing makeup and several strands of pearls. It's odd to see her all dressed up, wearing her jewelry. And then I notice she's wearing lots of other pieces as well— necklaces, bracelets, rings. Her pockets are weighed down with what looks like jewels. *Why is she wearing so much jewelry?*

"What she did to him?" Her voice has taken on an edge that's almost maniacal. "It's not what Charlotte did to Tucker. It's what *you* did to them."

I shake my head, willing it to make sense. Sure, Tucker and I had some chemistry when we met. But I made sure to keep it professional. He was engaged to someone else.

"What then? What did I do?" Anger tinges my voice, frustration taking over my desire to stay calm.

"Well, it's a rather long story, but I'll give you the short version." Amanda speaks in a composed, teacher-like tone. "Tucker and Charlotte had been having some trouble. The wedding was causing a bit of stress between them, and Tucker was unhappy. Charlotte refused to see it for what it was—he'd lost interest in her. The shiny veneer of her had started to wear off. This rift created an opening for him to be swayed toward someone else."

She pauses, her eyes boring into mine. "So, when I saw the way Tucker looked at you at the cake tasting that day, I knew. I knew you were going to be a problem. I knew that Tucker was attracted to you and he was already considering the idea of leaving my dear Charlotte. And that's exactly what happened."

I shake my head from side to side, confused. "No, Tucker and I didn't start dating until after the wedding was canceled."

"Oh, Reese, you're so naïve," Amanda says, her voice dripping with condescension. "Why do you think he kept stopping into your shop to buy cupcakes twice a week? Or take you out to lunch or for coffee whenever you were free? He was falling for you. Sure, you may not have had your first date until after the wedding never happened, you may not have shared your first kiss until a month later, but he was already smitten. He was already in love. I've been around long enough to know what it looks like."

She shifts her stance, moving the plastic gasoline can across the table. Several of her large gold and silver bracelets clang against the stainless steel, the sound echoing in the quiet kitchen. It crosses my mind that I could start screaming right now, but I know it's no use. It's Saturday morning, and all the shops are closed, including mine. Many of the shop owners next door are probably already at the wedding, seated on either the groom's or the bride's side of the aisle. I feel like I might throw up, but I manage to swallow hard.

I try to focus on what Amanda is saying, accusing me of having an affair with Tucker even though I was dating someone else and the two of them were nearly a month away from their wedding. At the same time, I'm not even sure what to say right now. It feels like she's made up her mind. Wearing all of her best jewelry, and with that crazy look in her eyes, it's clear. *She plans to burn this place down with the two of us in it.* The thought terrifies me.

I need to keep her talking. The longer she talks, the better chance I have of getting the hell out of here.

"Okay, fine. Tucker liked me. But I kept it professional. I would never—"

"Oh, drop the innocent little act, Reese. I'm not buying it. "

My mouth falls open. *How could she?*

"You're wrong. I was dating Zach. If I hadn't met Tucker, we'd probably still be together."

It felt wrong to admit it, but it was true. I liked Zach. *Really* liked him. Maybe I wasn't madly in love with him like I am with Tucker, but at the time, I didn't know any better.

Amanda tips her head back and begins to laugh.

"You really are clueless, Reese. Did Zach even tell you he was engaged before?"

My heart thuds in my chest. I shake my head, which is painful. At this point, I really don't care whom Zach dated, slept with, or was engaged to before. I want to get out of here. But the longer I keep her talking the better chance I have.

"No," I say.

She laughs again. "Well, I guess that doesn't surprise me. Zach was engaged to Charlotte. They dated for six years. He never got over the breakup. He was still calling and texting her, even when he was with you."

I swallow a lump in my throat, which is so incredibly

dry. It stings a little, knowing he wasn't completely honest. But then again, *neither was I*.

"They stayed friends, *even after they broke up*. Does that sound familiar?" She pauses and raises her eyebrows at me. "But, of course, it was different in your situation. Zach didn't want to stay friends with you—he was angry. Furious after what happened to Charlotte."

"Then why did he stay friends with me?" I ask, playing along. My eyes continue to flit around the room, searching for anything to get me out of this situation. Not to mention, the longer I keep her talking, the more time the driver has to return. *What is taking him so long?*

"Because I asked him to."

I turn my eyes back to her, the two of us locked in a long stare.

What is she talking about?

CHAPTER FORTY

My brain tries to play catch-up. It's impossible. I struggle against the restraints again. Amanda's wild eyes are staring at me, and I feel utterly terrified. The smell of gasoline is overwhelming, making my head spin. One side of my brain is in survival mode, looking for any possible way out of here. The other side is trying to process the fact that Zach stayed friends with me *because Amanda asked him to.*

"Why would you ask him to be friends with me after we broke up?"

Amanda gives a tiny shrug. "Simple. I wanted to keep tabs on you and Tucker. I thought for certain you would say no, as it wasn't exactly fair to Tucker. But you didn't. You lied to Tucker about Zach, all because you wanted to grow your little business." She looks around the room and rolls her eyes. "Really, you and Tucker deserve each other. It's all about greed and success with you two. But what you don't deserve? Is to have the life that was intended for my daughter."

I see it again, the terrifying flash of hatred passing across her eyes. *But she left Tucker!* I want to scream. But I see she has more to say, so I keep my mouth shut.

"Anyway, Zach has been a doll. He helped me set up a Snaptalk account so I could message you anonymously. He helped me break into your shop, bought me the spray paint to redecorate the front windows... He's been so helpful. Isn't that nice of him?"

Tears sting my eyes. *I trusted Zach.* I thought he was my friend. How could he do this to me?

"There, dear, don't cry. We haven't even gotten to the good part yet. It was Zach's idea to burn down your shop."

"Why?" I croak.

"Because he hates you. For what you did to him and Charlotte. He wanted her to be happy, even after she broke his heart. And then cheating on him, just when he was starting to fall for you? It was despicable." She narrows her eyes at me before continuing. "So, he sent a message pretending to be that little nitwit you employ, Bernie. It was easy to get your attention. All we had to do was send a message that your shop was on fire, and voilà, you're here."

Tears start to fall down my cheeks, despite my best effort. The zip ties bite into my wrists and ankles as I instinctively struggle against them, the rough plastic edges chafing my skin.

"Of course," she continues, her voice dripping with malice, "he didn't know I was planning on you burning up in flames along with this dumpy little bakery. He just wanted you to watch." Amanda's eyes are wild, pupils dilated with a manic gleam. "I didn't want him to get in trouble either, so I sent him off to that ridiculous gala while I get to revel in the last part of our plan."

She begins flipping the lighter lid open and closed,

creating a rhythmic *click, click, click.* Sweat trickles down my back, my dress sticking uncomfortably to my skin. The room's heat is stifling, intensifying the acrid smell of fear emanating from my pores. *What can I possibly say to stop her?*

"You don't have to do this, Amanda, really. I'm sorry, so sorry. Let me talk to Charlotte, tell her it's all a mistake."

She shakes her head and holds up her hand. "That's impossible."

My heart pounds so loudly I can hear it echoing in my ears. "Why?" I say.

She stops fidgeting with the lighter. Tears well up in her eyes and start running down her cheeks. The sudden vulnerability in her expression is jarring.

"Because Charlotte killed herself," she says, her voice barely above a whisper.

The news settles in, a cold weight in my stomach. *Charlotte...dead?* No, that can't be right. She left Tucker at the altar. She ran away. She's been living her life on a beach somewhere. Hasn't she? A wave of nausea hits me, and I taste bile in the back of my throat.

My thoughts race, memories flashing through my mind. *All this time, I thought... But she's been... How could I not have known? Did Tucker know?* The room starts to spin, and I blink rapidly, trying to focus on something, anything, to keep myself grounded.

"Charlotte's dead?" I ask, though as soon as I say it, it sounds hollow, dumb. My voice sounds distant, as if someone else is speaking. I can feel my pulse throbbing in my temples, a counterpoint to the burning in my wrists and ankles. The fluorescent lights overhead seem to flicker and dim, casting strange shadows across Amanda's face, transforming her once-familiar features into something alien and terrifying.

"Yes," she croaks.

"Why did she..."

Amanda seems to collect herself then, letting out a long sigh. Her eyes widen.

"Because of you," she spits.

"But Tucker and I didn't—"

"Oh, shut up. No one is buying that for a second, Reese. Charlotte knew about the two of you. She saw you together. She called me a couple of days before the wedding and told me. Poor Charlotte has always struggled with...stress. I put her in therapy as a child, which made some improvement, but high school was especially hard for her. I found the best doctors, got her the newest and best medications. She seemed to be managing everything just fine. But a few months before the wedding, she stopped taking her medication. I didn't realize until afterward, but...the stress of the wedding was just too much for her."

I try to take in everything she's saying, wiggling my wrists and ankles against the restraints. The heat from the room and the stress have made my skin wet with sweat. Maybe if I pull hard enough...

Amanda continues, seemingly oblivious to my struggles. "And then when she found out about you and Tucker, well, I think she snapped. The night before the wedding, she and Tucker agreed she was to stay at her condo in the city. He dropped her off there after the rehearsal dinner. A few hours later, she sent me a message uncharacteristic of her. It just said, 'I love you, Mother.'"

Amanda's bracelets jingle as she wipes a few tears from her cheeks. "I knew right away something was wrong. I jumped in my car and made the thirty-minute drive to her place in just twenty minutes. But by the time I got there, it was too late."

Her voice is wavering now, emotional. I think for a moment she might start to sob. I listen quietly, keep my eyes on her as I work my hands and feet against the restraints.

"I found her in her bathroom, wearing her wedding dress." Her voice falters then, and she starts to cry. She continues, her words punctuated by sobs. "She slit her wrists, and by the time I arrived, she was already gone."

I stop moving and stare at her. "Why didn't you tell anyone?"

Amanda pats her cheeks, then takes a shaky breath. Her eyes narrow in on me. "Tell anyone? And let her become the jewel of the town gossip? Taint her legacy...and mine?" She shakes her head. "I couldn't. So I called Zach. I knew he would understand. He...got rid of her body."

CHAPTER FORTY-ONE

I feel my body begin to tremble, a cold sweat breaking out across my skin. The realization hits me hard. *Zach covered up Charlotte's suicide. Disposed of her body? Hates me so much he helped Amanda set this whole thing up?* Tears well up, unbidden. I blink rapidly, trying to force them back, the salt stinging my eyes. The room seems to spin, and I struggle to focus.

"Amanda," I manage, my voice quavering, "I'm so sorry about Charlotte. It's awful, devastating. But this isn't the answer. Killing me won't bring her back to you."

Amanda's eyes flash with anger. "I know it won't. She's gone!"

I scan the room desperately, searching for any possible escape. The rough texture of the wooden chair digs into my arm, and suddenly I notice something—a slight give in the right armrest. I subtly wiggle and pull at the loose arm, feeling it give way slightly more with each tug.

I press on, desperate to reach her. "Would Charlotte

have wanted you to hide her suicide? To cover up her pain like it never existed?"

Amanda flinches, her grip on the lighter faltering for a moment. "I...I was protecting her memory."

"Were you?" I ask softly. "Or were you protecting yourself? The family image?"

"You don't understand." For a heartbeat, I see the real Amanda—a grieving mother, lost and confused. But then, as quickly as it appeared, the vulnerability vanishes. Her face hardens once more.

"Maybe I don't," I admit. "But think about what Charlotte would want. Would she want you to do this? To throw your life away?"

"You don't know what she would want," Amanda spits. "You didn't know her."

"I didn't know her, you're right. But I know this isn't what she would have wanted for you. If you would just let me go—"

She turns to me, her eyes now hard and glittering with rage. The transformation is terrifying.

"I will never let you leave," she snarls, her voice low and guttural. "You're going to die right here, in this bakery where you seduced my future son-in-law. You're going to pay for what you did. You're going to pay for Charlotte's death."

She pats the jewelry hanging around her neck. "That's why I'm here, wearing all my best jewels. You killed my daughter, so there's no one to inherit them now. Besides, I'd rather die on my own terms than set foot in one of those prisons."

As Amanda speaks, I continue to work at the loose chair arm, desperation lending me strength. If I can just break it free, I might have a chance... "Oh, Amanda, this isn't you.

You're a good person. You would never hurt me. I know it. Please, you have to let me go," I plead, my heart racing. "I won't marry Tucker if that's what you want. I'll cancel the wedding."

"Cancel the wedding?" she scoffs. "You expect me to believe that? If I let you go, all you'll do is turn me in to the police. You and Tucker will get me locked away for life, and then he'll turn around and marry you after all. No, this is exactly how it's going to go down. Charlotte was my only daughter, and you took her life away from her. Now I'm going to take yours." She flicks open the lid of the lighter.

With a final, desperate tug, the chair's right arm breaks with a loud crack. Amanda whirls around, her eyes widening in shock. With my right hand free, I waste no time fumbling for the zip tie around my ankles. The voluminous folds of my wedding dress stop me, tangling around my legs.

"No!" Amanda screams, lunging toward me.

I lose my balance, toppling sideways onto the slick floor. The sharp smell of gasoline assaults my nostrils as I hit the ground hard, the impact knocking the wind out of me. The chair shatters beneath me, finally allowing me to pull my legs free. A shard of the wood still dangles from my left wrist. Amanda is on me in an instant, her fingers clawing at my dress, trying to pin me down.

"You're gonna pay for what you did to her!" she shrieks, her face contorted with rage. "You took everything from me. My daughter, my future!"

I thrash wildly, my free hand searching for purchase on the slippery floor. My fingers brush against something solid— the leg of a prep table. I grab it, using it as leverage to pull myself away from Amanda's grasp.

With a surge of adrenaline, I manage to plant my left

foot against her chest and kick hard with my right. My heel connects with her face with a sickening thud. Amanda reels backward, blood streaming from her nose. She groans, her hand grasping at her face.

I scramble backward, trying to create as much distance between us as I can. That's when I notice it—the lighter, about ten feet away. Amanda must have dropped it when she came after me. I start moving toward it. She must have seen it too, because she lunges in the same direction.

Time slows down as I struggle forward, my vision blurring from the earlier blow to my head. The fall from the chair has left me disoriented, and my limbs feel leaden. Amanda, driven by her manic rage, reaches the lighter first. My heart plummets as her fingers close around it.

With trembling hands, she flicks it open. Desperation surges through me, and I summon every ounce of strength left in my body. Just as her thumb moves to ignite the flame, I lash out with my foot, connecting solidly. The lighter flies from her grasp, skittering across the slick floor toward the kitchen doorway.

We both scramble after it, slipping and sliding in the gasoline. The acrid fumes burn my lungs as I gasp for air, my wedding dress hampering my movements. Amanda, unencumbered, pulls ahead.

She snatches up the lighter, triumph glinting in her eyes as she turns to face me. Time slows to a crawl as I watch her thumb descend on the ignition wheel. A small flame springs to life, dancing in her crazed eyes.

A wicked, almost gleeful smile spreads across Amanda's face as she locks eyes with me. In that moment, I see no trace of the grieving mother—only a woman consumed by vengeance and madness.

"This ends now," she whispers, lowering the lighter toward the gasoline-soaked floor.

Terror grips me as I realize what's about to happen. I open my mouth to plead, to reason, to do anything to stop this madness, but all that comes out is a primal, desperate scream as the flames come to life, dancing across the floor.

It's only a matter of seconds before the hem of my wedding dress catches on fire.

CHAPTER FORTY-TWO

My entire world is in flames. I desperately paw at the flames licking up my dress, but it's useless. My eyes tear across the room, searching for help. Suddenly I spot the bright red fire extinguisher mounted on the wall. Searing pain overwhelms me as I desperately stumble toward it, panic rising in my throat.

I'm only a few feet away from the extinguisher, which is near the doorway to the hall, when I feel a tug at my dress. Amanda is behind me, her eyes wild, clawing at the hem of my dress. I reach back and try to swat her away but it's useless. She's pulling me back into the flames.

"Reese!"

I hear a voice ring out, so clear I nearly stop in my tracks. My mother is standing at the doorway to the kitchen, wearing a blue dress, her eyes wide. I blink twice to make sure I'm not imagining it.

"Mom, the fire extinguisher!" I scream, pointing toward the wall. Her eyes follow mine and with two quick movements she grabs the extinguisher and pulls it from the wall.

She closes the distance between us, aiming directly at my body. She rushes to me, aiming the nozzle and spraying. I manage to squeeze my eyes shut a split second before she douses me. The white foam hisses as it makes contact with the fire.

As Mom fights to put out the flames on my dress, Amanda, still on fire, charges toward her with a primal roar. In one fluid motion, Mom swings the fire extinguisher, connecting solidly with Amanda's head. The impact reverberates through the chaos, and Amanda crumples to the floor, unconscious. Mom sprays her down as well.

"Mom, how did you—?"

Before she has a chance to explain, I hear a whooshing sound from the corner of the room. The fire continues to spread, consuming everything in its path. Mom's face is a mask of determination as she empties the last of the extinguisher's contents onto me. Through the smoke and pain, I lock eyes with my mother. In that moment, I see a mix of fear, love, and fierce protectiveness. We both know we're running out of time.

"We need to get out of here, now!" Mom shouts, coughing from the thick smoke. She reaches for me, but I pull back.

"No, there's another fire extinguisher, in the hallway. If we can get to it—"

Even now, I can't imagine losing my shop. It's everything I have worked for. I can't—

"It's too late for that," she says, grabbing me by the arm. "We have to go. We have to go now," she insists.

"No," I argue, "we have to put this fire out. Come on!" I say, pulling her back into the bakery with me.

"Reese, please, we have to—"

A deafening crack interrupts her plea. We both look up to see a flaming rafter plummeting toward us. My mother yanks me back just as it crashes to the floor, sending a shower of sparks and embers into the air. The reality of the situation hits me like a physical blow. The heat intensifies, and I can hear the building groaning around us. My heart shatters as I realize the truth.

I have to let it go. I have to say goodbye to my shop. It's too late.

My eyes float down to the floor where Amanda's lying unconscious. "Come on," I say, "we have to get her. We can't leave her here."

"Okay," my mother says. The two of us each grab one of Amanda's legs and drag her out of the room as it becomes engulfed in flames. The smoke is rolling through the air now, thick and heavy. I can't stop coughing. Between the smoke and the tears burning my eyes it's difficult to see.

"This way!" I say to my mother as we drag Amanda down the hallway. The smoke rolls around us, so thick and heavy it's hard to see. We struggle to drag Amanda's limp body toward the front of the bakery. Every breath is a battle, the acrid smoke burning my lungs. We're mere feet from the lobby when a deafening boom shakes the building to its foundation.

The force of the explosion hurls us down the hallway like rag dolls. I crash into the doorway of the lobby and land behind the display counter. My ears ring from the blast as I struggle to orient myself. Mom lets out a pained cry beside me—she's pushed up against the wall, her face contorted in agony.

"My shoulder," she gasps through gritted teeth.

I can barely make out Amanda's body behind us, still in the hallway now filled with billowing black smoke. With strength I didn't know I had left, I grab Mom under her good arm and haul her toward the door.

Suddenly, a figure appears in the doorway, silhouetted against the smoke. It's Tucker, still in his wedding tux, his eyes bulging.

"Reese!" he screams, his voice hoarse.

"We can make it," I croak, my throat raw from the smoke. I point my arm behind us to the hallway, where Amanda's unconscious body is on the ground. "Get her!"

Without hesitation, Tucker plunges past us into the inferno. Mom and I stumble out, collapsing in a heap on the sidewalk. Agonizing seconds tick by, each moment stretching into eternity as I stare at the blazing doorway, silently willing Tucker to emerge.

Finally, he appears, carrying Amanda's limp form over his shoulder. Relief floods through me, so intense it's almost painful. He gently lays her on the ground, then turns to me, his eyes filled with concern.

"Are you okay?" he asks, kneeling beside me. I nod weakly, unable to speak. He pulls me into his arms, and I feel myself start to relax, gulping in the cool, clear air.

As the adrenaline begins to ebb, I become aware of the throbbing pain from burns and bruises. Mom clutches her injured shoulder, her face pale with shock. We lie there on the cold concrete, coughing and trying to catch our breath.

In the distance, I hear the wail of sirens growing louder. Fire trucks screech to a halt in front of the bakery, followed by police cars converging on the scene. As paramedics rush toward us and firefighters charge into the burning bakery, the full weight of what just happened begins to sink in. I turn to face my shop. The entire place is in flames. The heat sears my face as I watch my dreams go up in smoke, the acrid smell of burning filling the air. Tears stream down my face as I realize everything I've worked for is gone.

CHAPTER FORTY-THREE

"I told you I don't need to go to the hospital," I say to the paramedic for the third time, my voice hoarse from smoke inhalation.

It's been about forty-five minutes since it happened. Forty-five minutes since my entire shop went up in flames. I sit in the back of the ambulance as the sirens flash around me, casting eerie red and blue lights across the scene. The firefighters work their hoses; water sprays over the building with a hissing sound.

The once cheerful striped awning that framed the front is half burnt and flapping in the wind. The beautiful display windows are completely blown out, shattered glass glittering on the sidewalk. There are a few flames still licking the edges of the brick and limestone, but most of the fire has gone out. The roof has caved in, and it's now just a husk of what it was before.

I'm numb. Even as the paramedic next to me holds an ice pack on the side of my head, which has numbed the pain for the most part, it still feels as though my entire body is in shock. I can't quite put the thoughts together.

I watch Tucker standing in his tux, talking to the police. He was there at the very last minute, when it counted, when my mother and I needed help to get those last few steps outside the front door.

And he's here now, talking to the police, and checking on my mother, who sits in another ambulance across the street. They separated us for treatment when they arrived and I haven't had a chance to properly thank her for what she did. My mother, of all people, is the one who saved my life. How she beat Tucker to the shop is a story I hope to hear later. In the meantime, I am just incredibly grateful that she was here when I needed her. Sure, there have been many times in my life when she wasn't. But after today, I think I can let it slide.

Tucker suddenly turns to face me, his tuxedo tie hanging loosely around his neck. If anyone can help me rebuild the shop, I know it's him.

I just hope he can handle the news I'm about to tell him.

Despite my throbbing head, I smile. He nods to the police officer in front of him and then heads in my direction. A few seconds later, he's next to me, his arm wrapped around me as I sit on the stretcher in the back of the ambulance.

"I'll give you a few minutes," says the paramedic, stepping out of the back and walking around the side.

"How are you holding up?" Tucker asks, his voice gentle.

"I'm...I'm fine. Just..." I struggle to find the words. "It's just the shock of it all. It's just hard to believe that Amanda wanted me dead. That she burned down my shop."

I hold back tears. I gave Tucker the abbreviated version right before the ambulance arrived, but there is still so much more I have to tell him. I'm still having trouble matching up the thoughts in my head with the words that are coming out of my mouth, but the more I talk, the easier it seems to get. The paramedic said I didn't show any signs of a concussion, but I was to be monitored just in case.

"I know it's hard right now," he says, squeezing my hand. "The police want you to give a full statement, but I'm trying to give you as much time as I can. I told them you were still feeling lightheaded and confused."

"What about the wedding? Is everyone there waiting for us?" I ask, suddenly remembering the hundreds of guests we've left in limbo.

Tucker shakes his head. "Actually, Monica stepped in and took charge of the whole situation. She told everyone that there had been a fire at the bakery and you ran back to help. She's coordinating with Elsa, so you have nothing to worry about. I've been getting a few updates from her here and there. She promises that she'll take care of everything for us."

A little part of me relaxes. If anyone can handle this situation, it's Monica. It gives me a whole new appreciation for her.

"There's something I want to tell you," I say, my voice barely above a whisper.

He looks at me, his big eyes open and caring. I wish we weren't here in this moment. I wish instead I was looking at those eyes when we say our vows in front of a couple hundred friends and family. I lick my lips, tasting ash and smoke. I guess today wasn't meant to go like that.

"It's about Charlotte," I say.

In the past, he would've shut me down, gotten angry, or turned away. But in this moment, he sits there, his eyes still open. He takes a deep breath and lets it out slowly. "What is it?" he asks.

"Amanda told me what happened to Charlotte."

He raises his eyebrows. "Okay..."

I take a deep breath, steeling myself for what I'm about to say. "The night before the wedding, Charlotte was in her condo. And..." It's hard for me to say the next few words. I don't know how he's going to react, but I know he needs to know this now before anyone else finds out. "She committed suicide. She got in her bathtub and slit her wrists."

First, his eyes grow wide, and then narrow again. I see what appears to be tears creasing the corners of his almond-shaped eyes. He looks away from me for a few seconds. I place my hand on top of his.

He looks back at me, and I can see that he's emotional. He doesn't say anything, but he doesn't need to. His expression says it all.

"There's more," I continue softly. "Her mother found her in the bathroom. And Amanda was so worried, so ashamed, so concerned about what people would think...she covered it up. She called Zach, and he helped her get rid of the body before anyone knew what really happened."

I see his Adam's apple bob up and down as he swallows hard.

"Wow," he says quietly. "Zach? And Amanda told you all this?"

I nod. "She told me everything. She was planning on burning down the entire bakery with the two of us inside."

"And all those messages from Snaptalk? The spray paint on your shop?"

"Amanda and Zach."

Tucker's face suddenly darkens, his jaw clenching. "I'm

going to kill him," he growls, his hands balling into fists. "How dare he put you through this?"

I place a calming hand on his arm. "Tucker, please. It's not worth it. The police will take care of him."

He takes a deep breath, visibly trying to control his anger. "Why would Zach help her?"

"He was angry that I cheated on him with you. But more than that, I guess he still loved Charlotte. After all this time. And he blamed me for what she did, killing herself. They both did."

Tucker shakes his head. "Reese, that was not your fault. You did nothing wrong. We didn't—"

"I know. But...they didn't see it that way."

Tucker shakes his head and wraps his arm around me. "I can't believe that she covered up suicide...that Zach helped her. Why would she do that?"

"Like I said, she was worried about what people would think."

Tucker rubs his chin. "I know that Charlotte had some problems, that she had seen a therapist, but she assured me that everything was fine. She was on medication."

I nod. "Amanda told me the same thing. She also told me that Charlotte had stopped taking her meds a couple of months before the wedding."

He shakes his head again, taking his thumb and forefinger to rub his eyes and the bridge of his nose. "I can't believe that. I can't believe after all this time I thought that she left me at the altar out of spite, out of some hatred that she had for me because..." He pauses, letting his voice drift off.

"Because of what?" I ask gently.

He looks me in the eyes again. "Because she thought we

were having an affair. And to be honest, I did have feelings for you, but I would've never done that to Charlotte. I loved her—not in the way that I love you, but what I thought was enough at the time. I dropped her off at the condo that night. She confronted me about you, and I tried to break things off. But she broke down, begged me to reconsider." Tears well up in his eyes again. "I thought maybe she was right, maybe I just had cold feet. And despite my growing feelings for you, nothing had happened between us yet. I did love her at one time. Maybe I could again. I agreed to go through with the wedding, even though I knew it was wrong. She must have sensed it, that it was doomed from the start. And then... I didn't know she would..."

I lean into him and wrap my fingers around his. "You couldn't have known, Tucker. You couldn't have known what she was going to do."

The two of us sit in silence, watching the lights blink and flash around us. In the time that we've been talking, all of the flames have disappeared from the bakery, and now it's just smoke and steam rising up into the early evening sky. I take the ice pack that I've been pressing against my head and set it down on the gurney.

I stare at the group of police standing on the sidewalk, waiting for my statement. The gravity of Amanda's confessions and Zach's involvement presses heavily on my conscience. Part of me yearns to spill everything, to finally bring the truth about Charlotte's death to light. Amanda and Zach should face the full consequences for their actions, right? But doubt creeps in. Will the police believe me? Without concrete evidence, it's my word against theirs.

Then I think about Charlotte, how she never received a proper funeral. How her friends never had a sense of closure about her disappearance. *It's not my secret to bear.* Taking a deep breath, I make my decision. I'll tell the police everything. It's time for the secrets to end, for the truth to come out, no matter how messy or painful. Whatever happens next, at least I'll know I did the right thing.

"I think I'm ready to talk to the police now," I say. I squeeze his hand. "Will you be all right?"

Tucker looks me in the eyes. "As long as I know you're okay, I'll be fine," he says. "I love you."

"I love you too."

CHAPTER FORTY-FOUR

SIX MONTHS LATER

I pause from frosting the two-tiered cake in front of me and stare at the wedding band on my finger. The crystal-clear diamonds sparkle under the ceiling lights. It's been two months since Tucker and I finally walked down the aisle, and I'm still getting used to it.

Being Mrs. Tucker Harding.

I can't believe it finally happened. After all the drama, the threats, the near-death experiences—we actually did it. And you know what? *It was perfect.*

After everything that went down, Tucker and I decided the best way to get married was to elope. We organized a quick beach wedding in Cabo San Lucas, just the two of us, saying our vows with the ocean waves rolling in and out behind us. No crazed almost-mothers-in-law, no arsonist ex-boyfriends, no family drama.

Just us, the sand, and the setting sun.

"Reese? Are you ready for the fondant?" I hear Bernie call from across the room.

We're working at a commissary kitchen about three

blocks away from the bakery. I'm relieved to say that we'll only be here for a few more weeks. The insurance settlement that came in after the fire was more than I expected. In fact, I don't even know why I hesitated and tried to put the flames out when I was wrestling with Amanda. I'll be able to rebuild the shop even better than it was before. No flea market finds or hand-me-down ovens.

Although that flea market chair did come in handy.

The bell above the kitchen door chimes, and I look up from where I'm working to see Monica striding in. My face breaks into a genuine smile when I see her carrying two paper cups.

"Monica! What a surprise," I say, wiping my hands on my apron.

She grins, her perfectly styled hair bouncing as she walks. "I was just down the road at Marla's and thought I'd drop by with some caffeine. Latte, extra hot, right?"

I wince slightly. Afternoon lattes at Marla's was something I used to share with... I catch myself. *Not a good time to think about him.*

"You remembered," I say, forcing a smile. "Thank you. This is exactly what I needed."

Monica leans against the counter, her eyes scanning the kitchen. "The bakery looks like it's coming along nicely. Any updates on when you will reopen?"

"A few weeks."

"Wonderful," she says. A comfortable silence falls between us as we sip our drinks. It's a far cry from the tension-filled moments we used to share. At least for me. I don't think Monica has ever felt uncomfortable in her life.

When our original wedding was postponed, Monica stepped in and worked wonders. There was no way Tucker and I could have managed the investigation and the wedding vendors at the same time. I was right when I assumed that she'd be able to handle things with a deft touch. She, along with Elsa, managed to rework arrangements with each of the vendors—the food, the band, everything. And after we returned from Cabo, she threw us a surprise wedding reception. It was tasteful and small, just perfect. Monica takes a little getting used to, but I am so grateful for everything she did.

"You know," I say, breaking the silence, "I never properly thanked you for that surprise reception you threw us when we got back from Cabo."

Monica waves her hand dismissively, but I can see the pleasure in her eyes. "Oh, please. After everything you two have been through? It was the least I could do."

"It meant so much to us, Monica. Really. I know we didn't always see eye to eye, but that reception...it meant a lot to me."

Monica's eyes soften. "Well, you're one of us now, Reese. Whether you like it or not," she adds with a wink. She takes a deep breath, as if steeling herself. "I have to admit something. When you and Tucker first got together, I was...skeptical."

Gee, Monica, I couldn't tell.

"Really?" I say, feigning surprise.

"It wasn't just because of how quickly it happened," Monica continues. "Tucker's my cousin, and I've always felt protective of him. After Charlotte...well, I was scared he was rushing into something he wasn't ready for."

"I understand," I say softly. "I had my own doubts too in the beginning."

Monica reaches out and squeezes my hand. "But, Reese,

you proved me wrong. You proved everyone wrong. The way you stood by Tucker through everything, how you've integrated into the family, how you two support each other...it's clear how much you love him."

I feel tears pricking at the corners of my eyes. "I do love him. So much."

"I know that now," Monica says, her voice thick with emotion. "And I'm so glad you're a part of our family. I'm sorry if I ever made you feel unwelcome."

I shake my head, squeezing her hand back. "That's all in the past. What matters is where we are now."

Monica smiles, raising her latte. "To family?"

I clink my cup against hers. "To family."

"I should get going," she says, standing up. "See you tomorrow?"

"Yes," I say. "Looking forward to it."

If you would have told me a year ago I'd be playing tennis every week with Monica and her country club crew, I wouldn't have believed it. But here we are, and times have indeed changed. Word is, Monica's a beast on the court—all fierce backhands and killer serves. Little does she know I was on the all-star tennis team in high school. Guess we'll see who's queen of the court now.

I sigh, and return to the cake in front of me. The shock of everything has settled, for the most part. Tucker has insisted I go and talk to someone—a therapist—to help me work through what happened. I've found that seeing someone has really helped me process all of it.

Thankfully, I'll never have to see Amanda Spencer or Zach Caldwell ever again. Amanda was initially charged with arson and attempted first-degree murder, which could have meant life in prison. But the case took an unexpected turn.

During the pre-trial proceedings, Amanda's lawyer argued for an insanity plea, citing the profound trauma of her daughter's suicide as the catalyst for her actions. Psychiatric evaluations revealed the extent of her mental breakdown.

In the end, the prosecution agreed to a plea deal. Instead of prison time, Amanda was sentenced to involuntary commitment in a high-security psychiatric facility. She'll undergo intensive therapy and treatment for an indefinite period, with regular evaluations to determine if she's ever fit to re-enter society. It's not the outcome I expected, but in a way, it feels right. Amanda needs help more than punishment. And while part of me still fears her, I hope she finds peace and healing.

As for Zach? I haven't seen him since the night he broke into my shop. Once his involvement in the plot to burn down my shop and the rest came to light, Tucker insisted the police put a restraining order in place. Of course, I'd love to punch him in the face after everything he did to me, but knowing he'll go to prison is enough for now.

The police are still gathering evidence for his trial. Amanda confessed everything as part of her plea deal, but Zach has been more defiant. Forensic analysts have combed through his electronic devices, uncovering deleted messages and location data that contradict his alibi the night of the suicide. Not to mention the fact that he had logged into Charlotte's social media accounts several times to post on her behalf after she died. From what I've heard, they are still tracking down witnesses who might have seen Zach in areas near the coast where he's suspected of disposing of the body in the ocean.

The thought still gives me shivers.

I've already given my testimony—which is basically what Amanda told me—so I should be minimally involved from here on out. I had no idea that Zach had ever been engaged to Charlotte, much less covered up her suicide. It's chilling to think about how little we know about the people in our lives.

Sometimes I still think about Charlotte. It seems profoundly sad that she died the way she did and no one will even memorialize her loss. She was a person with dreams, fears, people who loved her. She deserves to be remembered as more than just a victim in a tragic story. I hope her mother does something for her, but given Amanda's mental state, I'm not sure that will happen.

My phone buzzes, and I see my mother's name on the caller ID. A warm feeling spreads through my chest as I answer.

"Hi, Mom. How are you doing?"

"Oh, sweetheart, I'm doing just fine," she replies, her voice sounding stronger than it has in years. "This place you set me up in is really something. The staff here is wonderful."

I smile to myself. After everything that happened, I decided to move her closer to me here in Somerville. I subleased her my old apartment, which she'll be moving into after she gets through rehab. Tucker helped me throughout the process, even hired movers to have her belongings delivered to her new place.

"I'm so glad to hear that," I say, tucking the phone between my shoulder and ear. "How's your treatment going?"

"It's challenging, but I'm making progress every day." There's a pause, and then she continues, her voice softer. "Reese, I...I just wanted to thank you again. For everything. I know I haven't always been there for you, but—"

"Mom, I'm the one who should be thanking you. I don't know what I would have done if you hadn't shown up at my shop during the fire. I don't know how you knew..."

"A mother always knows," she says. I can almost hear her smile over the phone. "I also know how much you love that bakery and how hard you worked to make your dream a reality. So if there was a reason you'd miss out on your wedding, I figured it had to be something to do with Couture Cakes."

I open my mouth to thank her as my eyes well up with tears. But before I can answer, my mother interrupts.

"Oops, I have to run. We have a yoga class at three. Call you next week?"

"Of course. Love you, Mom."

"Love you too."

I drop the phone back on the work table, refocusing my energy on what's in front of me. My therapist says dwelling on the past isn't going to help me focus on the future, and that's where I'm most excited.

After everything that happened, I've decided that when I do reopen the shop, I'm going to try to take a more balanced approach. Bernie and I have already interviewed some new staff members to help manage the workload. I want to take a step back and focus on the family that Tucker and I will be building together soon.

"I'm ready for the fondant!" I call after Bernie.

But in the meantime, I've got a wedding cake to finish.

EPILOGUE

"Handle it, Brian," I say, gripping the phone until my knuckles turn white. "I know you can. You've already done it before; this time isn't any different. I want him buried. Completely."

"Yes, Mr. Harding. I'll make it happen," he replies.

Brian, one of my very highly paid lawyers, is getting me out of a tight situation with one of my business partners, Sergei. I think back on how the whole mess started. Sergei, that idiot, got caught reselling the counterfeit handbags I had imported. It was supposed to be a simple operation—I bring in the knockoffs, he moves them through his network of boutiques and online stores, and we all profit. But Sergei got sloppy, selling to an undercover agent who'd been tipped off about the counterfeit goods.

Now he's singing like a canary, trying to save his own skin by dragging my name into it. He's already tried to turn me in to the police, spinning some tale about how I'm the mastermind behind the whole operation. Little does Sergei know, I'm always ten steps ahead.

I cover my tracks meticulously. The paper trail is a maze of shell companies and offshore accounts. Even if the authorities could follow it, they'd hit nothing but dead ends. The only way to take me down is if someone had real proof, like actual video footage of our warehouse receiving goods. Which is why Charlotte was such a threat.

Anyway, I've got some of the best lawyers in the state working on this. Brian will come through, if he wants to be considered one of the best.

I lower my voice slightly as I continue. "Regarding the situation with Zach, are we making any progress?"

"The recording has been delivered, just in time for the last day of the trial," Brian replies.

My jaw clenches. *About damn time.* The memory of Zach threatening Reese flashes through my mind, igniting a fresh wave of anger. I take a deep breath, trying to keep my voice steady.

"Good. And there's no way to trace it back to us?"

"Nope. My guy has it locked up tight."

It better be. So far, Zach's team of slick, high-priced lawyers has been dancing circles around the prosecution. They've exploited every legal loophole—motions to suppress, claims of improper police procedure, character witnesses singing Zach's praises. They're pulling out all the stops.

They even managed to get DNA evidence found in his car thrown out on a technicality, leaving the prosecution scrambling. The thought of Zach walking free on some legal sleight of hand, potentially coming after Reese again, makes my blood boil.

"He better," I growl. "Because if anyone finds out, I won't be taking the fall alone. Understand?"

"Completely, Mr. Harding. I assure you—"

I cut him off. "I don't want assurances. I want results. This needs to be airtight. Zach goes away for good, end of story."

"Of course, sir. We're doing everything—"

I hang up without waiting for my lawyer to finish. *Let him sweat a little.* If he can't handle this, I'll find someone who can.

A knock at the door sends me straight up in my seat. Reese pokes her head in.

"Hey, honey. I'm heading to bed. Will you be up soon?"

I smile, covering up my surprise. *If she heard me talking to Brian...*

"I'll be right there. Just have to finish up a couple of emails."

"Okay, no worries," she says as she steps back into the hallway.

I stare after her for a moment. She couldn't have heard me. The door to my office is thick enough to muffle any sound, not to mention the extra lining I had installed around the door for privacy.

I lean back in my leather armchair and trace the intricate stitching on the armrests. It was a gift from Charlotte during one of her redecorating frenzies. I have to admit, she had a knack for it. Exquisite taste that matched her blue-blood upbringing. It was one of the things that initially drew me to her like a moth to a flame.

Unfortunately, looks can be deceiving.

When we first met, Charlotte seemed perfect. She was vivacious, charming, the life of every party. Everyone loved her—or so it seemed. My cousin Monica tried to warn me about Charlotte's instability, but I brushed it off. I was in my early thirties, riding high on business success, and eager to start a family. Charlotte, fresh from her breakup with Zach, seemed like the perfect fit.

Little did I know what lay beneath that polished exterior.

Behind closed doors, Charlotte was a different person entirely. Desperate for attention, cripplingly insecure—it would take her hours to get ready for a simple dinner out. The medication she was on when we started dating had masked these issues, but as time went on, her true nature emerged.

By the time I realized the extent of her mental problems, it was too late. We were mere months away from the wedding, and her mother, Amanda Spencer—a true leech if I've ever met one—was sinking her claws deeper into our lives and my wallet.

I should've known better. Should've seen that it was too good to be true. But the invitations had gone out, the deposits had been made. Everyone I knew, that my parents knew, was coming to the wedding. I was willing to go through with it all just to save face.

Then I met Reese.

It hit me like a freight train—this is what love feels like. Reese was everything Charlotte wasn't—equally beautiful, but with an underlying grit that commanded respect. She had substance, depth, a fire in her eyes that made my heart race in a way it never had before. I wanted to break up with Charlotte, but we were so close to the wedding that it felt impossible.

And then the night before our wedding, she confronted me about my business—had the audacity to threaten me with evidence. *Did she really think that I was going to let her control me the way her mother controlled her?* I knew I had to get rid of her, and with her history of depression and cutting, staging a suicide seemed like a perfect fit. In fact, with those razors sitting on her bathroom counter, it was almost too easy.

I had no idea the lengths that Charlotte's mother would go to cover it all up. And Zach? I thought I had gotten him off Charlotte's scent a long time ago. But he was clearly still in love with her, so much so that he was willing to hide her suicide.

I lean back, a wry smile playing on my lips as I recall the events that unfolded. When he disposed of her body in the ocean, Zach made a huge mistake. He chose a spot barely a mile down the road from my warehouse. A place where I had cameras. One of my security guys was watching the screen when it happened and promptly reported back to me. I decided to keep this recording close to my chest. There was no benefit in drawing attention to myself regarding her death, not when I had plausible deniability served on a silver platter. This turn of events made my situation infinitely cleaner. A suicide investigation might have led to some uncomfortable questions, potentially landing me in hot water. But everyone believing that Charlotte had cold feet and left me standing at the altar? Now that was a different story entirely.

Sure, the embarrassment stung for a while. The pitying looks, the whispered conversations that would abruptly halt when I entered a room. But it was a small price to pay for my freedom. After all, what's a bruised ego compared to a life sentence?

In the end, Charlotte's disappearance became nothing more than fodder for society gossip. And me? I emerged as the jilted groom, garnering sympathy instead of suspicion.

Sometimes, the best move is to play the victim, even when you're the one holding all the cards.

Of course, everything changed when Zach came after my fiancée. He crossed a line he can never uncross. Now, it's not just about justice—it's personal. I had to rethink my entire strategy. It was a risk, sharing the recording of him dumping Charlotte's body in the ocean. But it would be enough to send him to prison for good.

A buzzing from my phone breaks into my thoughts. It's my warehouse manager, calling *again*. I know what that means. I slam my fist on the desk and curse out loud.

A few seconds later, Reese pokes her head into the room.

"Babe?" she asks, her eyes concerned. "Is everything alright?"

"It's nothing, love. Just work, nothing major. I'll come to bed in a minute." She nods and I listen as her footsteps climb the stairs to the bedroom.

I pick up my phone with a sigh. God, I hope Reese never finds out about my business. Even if she did, I don't think she would blackmail me like Charlotte. Reese is different. Smarter. More curious. Would she understand? Maybe. If not? I'd have to make her see reason. Explain things. After all, she's not Charlotte. She's... important. I can't lose her. But I can't let her expose everything either. I'd find a way to deal with it. Carefully. Delicately.

After all, two suicides might seem suspicious.

ABOUT THE AUTHOR

Leah Cupps is a Multiple-Award Winning Author and Entrepreneur. She writes Thriller, Mystery, and Suspense as well as Middle-Grade Mystery Adventure Books.

Leah's novels are fast-paced thrillers that will keep you up at night as you can't wait to see what happens in the next chapter.

Leah lives in Indiana with her husband and three children. When she isn't losing sleep writing her next novel or scaling her next business, she enjoys reading, riding horses, working out, and spending time with her family.

Did you enjoy *Sweet Little Lies*? Please consider leaving a review on Amazon to help other readers discover the book.

Visit Leah Cupps on her website: www.leahcupps.com

ALSO BY LEAH CUPPS

One Last Bite
You Are Not Alone
Sweet Little Lies

Printed in Great Britain
by Amazon

57015361R00162